"Come here."

Leon's request—command, really—was impossible to ignore. Ettie was drawn to him. She had been from the first moment she'd seen him. So now she went to him, her heart thundering faster with every step.

"You're sure about this, Ettie?" he asked.

"Just this once," she whispered. "Only this once, okay?"

Leon didn't reply. He was so very still, so very serious. She knew he was thinking—she just didn't know what. But she sensed his tension, some kind of warring within. Instinctively, she reached out and placed her hand on his chest. His heart echoed hers—galloping, too. The pace reverberated through her palm, up her arm and into her own tightly wired body.

His enigmatic gaze glittered down at her. And then he smiled.

USA TODAY bestselling author **Natalie Anderson** writes emotional contemporary romance full of sparkling banter, sizzling heat and uplifting endings—perfect for readers who love to escape with empowered heroines and arrogant alphas who are too sexy for their own good.

When she's not writing, you'll find Natalie wrangling her four children, three cats, two goldfish and one dog...and snuggled in a heap on the sofa with her husband at the end of the day.

Follow her at www.natalie-anderson.com.

Books by Natalie Anderson

Harlequin Presents

Claiming His Convenient Fiancée
The Forgotten Gallo Bride
The King's Captive Virgin
Awakening His Innocent Cinderella

One Night With Consequences

Princess's Pregnancy Secret

The Throne of San Felipe

The Secret That Shocked De Santis
The Mistress That Tamed De Santis

Visit the Author Profile page
at Harlequin.com for more titles.

Natalie Anderson

PREGNANT BY THE COMMANDING GREEK

HARLEQUIN PRESENTS®

Recycling programs
for this product may
not exist in your area.

ISBN-13: 978-1-335-47828-3

Pregnant by the Commanding Greek

First North American publication 2019

Printed in U.S.A.

PREGNANT BY THE COMMANDING GREEK

For Kathleen, your relentless perseverance and efforts are such an inspiration to me—you rock!

CHAPTER ONE

'WHAT DO YOU MEAN, he wants us to "get rid of it"?' Antoinette Roberts scooped up the small, greying terrier and clutched him close. 'Doesn't he realise that "it" is a gorgeous, living creature?' She glared at Joel, her junior colleague.

'I don't think he does, Ettie,' Joel answered in an agitated whisper. 'He just stormed in here first thing and demanded access to Harold's apartment and started clearing stuff out.'

'You're kidding?' Disgust surged through Ettie.

Cavendish House, an exclusive apartment building in the heart of London's Mayfair, offered full concierge service to its privacy-loving residents, and, as head concierge, Ettie was used to delivering it for her demanding guests; from everyday mundane queries to the most outrageous, extravagant requests.

She didn't just arrange parcel deliveries and make restaurant bookings, she sourced rare first editions of famous novels and cajoled Michelin chefs to cook in a resident's apartment to help create the perfect proposal... And she was proud of the service she worked hard to provide. Until today there'd been no request she hadn't been able to fulfil.

But she drew the line at the euthanasia of a perfectly healthy, beloved pet on a total stranger's *whim*.

'I suppose George let him in?' she growled.

Joel nodded.

That'd be right. George, the building manager, was obsequious to clients, pernickety with petty rules while sloppy with what was actually crucial, and a belligerent bully to the personnel. Ettie spent half her time fixing his blunders and soothing staff resentment when he'd blamed them.

It was her fault it had got this far with the dog. She'd arrived late for the first time in years because she'd been up most of the night counselling her stressed-out sister, Ophelia, who was panicking that she'd flunked her latest physics test. Not that Ophelia had flunked a test in her life. Fiendishly academic, she was away at boarding school on a partial scholarship. Ettie was paying the rest of the fees and Ophelia was desperate to secure a university place. That meant another scholarship, which in turn meant outstanding results in every assessment in this last year of her schooling. As amazing as Ophelia was, Ettie worried the pressure was too intense. But she wouldn't let Ophelia give up her dream. Ettie had sacrificed too much herself to allow that. So, after calming Ophelia, she'd lain awake fretting about how she could better financially support her. Since their mother's death two years ago, it fell to Ettie to make it happen.

But making things happen was what Ettie did. She'd learned and worked for it, making miles-long lists and instituting systems so her sometimes impulsive and distraction-prone self wouldn't forget anything. But today she'd lapsed into her natural disorder. She'd overslept, in her mad scurry she'd missed breakfast, lost her last hair tie and resorted to using an old rubber band, and still missed her train.

When she'd finally raced into Cavendish House this morning, it was to the shocking news that her favourite long-term resident, Harold Clarke, had been rushed to hospital in the small hours of the night. While his passing had been quick and peaceful, his family—the family Ettie hadn't seen visit once in the five years she'd been working there—was already on the premises and clearing out his treasures. Apparently they didn't regard Toby, Harold's small terrier, as a treasure. They'd sent him down for Joel, her junior concierge, to "get rid of".

If Ettie had been at work on time, that nephew would never have made it into the apartment, let alone cast his callous instructions for Toby.

'Ettie, there's something else…' Joel called after her.

Not now there wasn't.

Shock, grief and sheer fury overrode the caution and calm she'd schooled within herself over the years. Ettie tightened her hold on the small dog and impulsively swept to the lift. Appalled by that uncaring request, she'd no time for niceties or other distractions. The family were monsters.

At the slide of the doors, Ettie stepped out onto Harold's floor. His apartment door was open and curt voices echoed along the corridor. She stalked the length of it, unconsciously stroking the soft fur of the small dog. A quick glance into the room showed George on the far side looking as smarmy as ever, next to an older-looking couple. All three were facing a tall man who had his back to her but, given the sullen looks on the faces of the others and the iceberg-thick atmosphere, he wielded the power. His immaculate appearance and crisply clipped hair enraged her all the more. He was obviously loaded because the impeccably tailored suit was clearly bespoke. No off-the-rack number ever fitted so perfectly—lovingly emphasising his height and strength. Though most men didn't have perfect physiques either. One look and she knew he was fit, healthy and wealthy. So why did he need to be so greedy over Harold's assets? Why be so *cruel*?

'You shouldn't be in here.' Ettie didn't hesitate stepping into the room.

How could he not have visited Harold in all this time and yet turn up the second he thought there were valuable possessions to be claimed?

'You don't storm in here and start stripping out Harry's assets and condemning his dog to instant death.' She barely paused to draw breath. 'You want to us to "get rid of" Toby?' Her voice quivered but she stood straight, not letting the tremble in her knees spread to the rest of her.

Because the man had turned around and Ettie was rendered breathless. He was much taller than her and younger than she expected. No older than thirty. But it was his face that stopped her—he had the sharpest, most handsome face she'd ever seen. High cheekbones, a straight nose, a full mouth, a cleft in his chin and a square, relentlessly masculine jaw…and to cap it off, deep brown, unbearably intense eyes. Brown eyes usually held some warmth, right? Not his. She'd never encountered either such beauty or such coldness. He was totally intimidating.

But it seemed he wasn't left as much breathless as speechless. Good. It was obviously time someone challenged him and his appalling instructions. Inhaling sharply, Ettie recovered enough to continue her attack.

'Toby is the sweetest little dog ever, not that you'd know because you never visited him or Harold in all this time…' Her voice trembled as she thought of the quiet elderly man who'd been gentle. And so alone. 'Now it's barely five minutes after…and you want Toby put down? Are you even human?'

George cleared his throat. 'Ettie—'

'You're not going to get away with it,' she carried on passionately, too steamed up to let George and his lack of spine stop her from telling this jerk some home truths. 'I won't let you.'

She became aware Joel had arrived and was breathlessly standing beside her, an appalled but fascinated expression on his face. The older couple present didn't look at her at all but stared at the tall stranger with silent, seething resistance. She knew how they felt.

The man's arctic glare sharpened on her, pinning her with almost visceral force. 'Who are you?'

She refused to quake. 'I think that's my question. You're the one trespassing.'

'I think not,' he said softly. There was a faint foreign tone to his cutting, cold accent.

George was frantically doing some kind of dance behind the arrogant ass's back. But she paid no attention—she was too incensed. The guy needed to be schooled. Tired and strung out and sad, Ettie couldn't hold back her contempt. 'You've never once set foot in this place before now.'

'No.' His quiet confirmation sounded stronger than George's audible gasp.

'You're despicable,' Ettie told him.

'Despicable?' He glanced behind him and caught George midway through miming self-strangulation. He turned back to face her. 'I think what your colleague is trying to convey is that you've made a mistake.'

There was the slightest curl to the man's lips—as if he was deriving some small, hideous pleasure from this moment.

Ettie frowned, not comprehending. She was still puffed from the force of her emotions and her furious dash up to the apartment. 'I'm not Mr Clarke's nephew,' he informed her with brutally cold precision. 'In fact, I'm no relation whatsoever to Mr Clarke.'

Nonplussed, Ettie blinked. Now she took a moment to study him, he didn't look anything like Harold. This man's hair was dark and thick and his eyes were that wintry brown, not blue, and his bronze complexion was more than a summer tan. A wave of relief so strong it was shocking rippled through her. He wasn't an animal-murdering brute?

Then she was hit with a wave of something else altogether. Something from deep inside, so hot and intense that she refused to acknowledge, let alone define it. Because it was *shocking*.

'Then what are you doing in here?' she snapped uncharacteristically. But she was determined to halt the appallingly inappropriate, *intimate* direction of her thoughts. Why was everyone looking at him as if he was ridiculously important? Why was George turning greener by the second?

'You've made a mistake.' His gaze drifted over her uniform in an inspection so quick it was almost insulting. 'And yet I think you're this star concierge I've heard about. Cavendish House's very own Girl Friday.'

She had a sudden prickling sensation that a giant black hole had opened up before her, but that she'd already taken the fatal step. It was too late to stop—the fall was in play and there was no way to backpedal and stop herself tumbling into a bottomless pit.

'My name is Leon Kariakis. And as of close of business last night, I own this building.'

Leon Kariakis? *The* Leon Kariakis? Serious, publicity-averse, wealthier-than-most-small-countries Leon Kariakis?

Ettie stared at him, slack-jawed. Oh, yeah, she'd fallen into one never-ending crevasse. All she could do was comment stupidly, 'You own…' she drew in a breath and tried to regroup '…and you're not—'

'No relative. This man is Mr Clarke's nephew and I've already spoken to him and his wife about Mr Clarke's belongings. Nothing will leave this building until the executor of his will has been to the premises and itemised everything.'

The other man began to bluster but Leon Kariakis turned and quelled him with a filthy look. 'Is it true you instructed the staff to get rid of the dog?'

The nephew didn't respond.

'Is it true?' Leon Kariakis demanded an answer.

'I didn't mean—'

'Evidently it was very clear what you meant.' Leon cut the man off. 'You will leave immediately.'

'You can't throw us out.'

'I think you'll find I can,' Leon Kariakis replied softly. The atmosphere chilled even more, his physical threat apparent even though he didn't move an inch. If Leon Kariakis wanted to manhandle this guy out of the apartment, he'd do so with ease. And the sorry excuse for Harold's family knew it.

Ettie's heart raced faster than a puppy chasing a pigeon. Since when was Cavendish House even on the market? And to be bought by Leon Kariakis? Even she'd heard of the serious son of the incredibly rich Kariakis holiday empire. His parents owned a number of swanky five-star hotels on the continent, but sole heir Leon had gone into finance, making even more eye-watering amounts of money in an unseemly short amount of time. Apparently buying up exclusive residential apartment buildings was his new hobby. And she'd just called him out—accusing him of animal cruelty and disgusting greed.

'This isn't over, Kariakis,' the nephew blustered. 'You'll be hearing from our lawyers.'

'I look forward to it,' Leon replied tersely. 'I imagine they'll be much more pleasant to deal with than you.'

Ettie bit down on her lip to stop her unbidden smile as the nephew and his wife stomped out of Harold's apartment. They didn't so much as look at her, or the small dog she was still cuddling. But neither she nor Toby were out of the woods yet. All-powerful, superserious, still scowling, Leon Kariakis wouldn't have appreciated her shouting at him in public like that.

'Everyone else, please leave as well.' He seared her with an icy glance. 'Except you.'

Yeah, she'd just lost her job.

George stepped in. 'Mr Kariakis, I'm terribly sorry for this misunderstanding. Ettie is always—'

'I'll meet with you later.' Leon Kariakis's snappy dismissal brooked no argument.

George shot her an irritated look that she ignored, even though she knew he'd been about to throw her even further under the bus. She was fine. She could handle it. But her heart thudded as her Joel reluctantly left too.

She turned to face the music, disconcerted to discover Leon Kariakis was still watching her and still wasn't smiling. Indignation surged and she lifted her chin at him. She'd been doing her job—protecting her client's pet—and she wasn't going to apologise for that. The silence echoed in the apartment. Even Toby, the dog, didn't stir in her arms, but she stroked him regardless.

'You're Antoinette Roberts,' he said quietly. 'Cavendish's Girl Friday. I've heard much about you and yet...'

She'd disappointed him?

Too bad. Even though she knew she was about to lose her job, she felt a small flush of pride that he'd been told about her. What had he said before—star concierge? Yet she couldn't claim any praise as entirely her own. Joel and the other guys were always willing to help.

'I have a very good team,' she said.

He kept regarding her steadily, but no warmth softened his eyes.

She should probably apologise for mistaking him for one of Harry's mean relatives, but suddenly she couldn't get her voice to work. Awareness trickled down her spine as the tension within her transformed. She'd loathed him on sight, only now...it was another emotion stiffening her spine. And it was just insane. Ettie Roberts did *not* lust after anyone. Ettie Roberts was far too sensible.

But Leon Kariakis was abnormally handsome and the way he was looking at her right now was unbearably intense. It was only that, mixed with relief that he wasn't a cruel tyrant out to murder an innocent animal, that made him all the more attractive in this moment, right? It wasn't *real*. Leon Kariakis wasn't someone she'd ever be interested in and he'd certainly never be interested in her.

A sudden wave of defensiveness let her mouth slip the leash. 'If you're going to sack me, just get it over with.'

There was another moment of profound silence. She burned with a horrible mix of embarrassment, nerves and resentment. She hated how calm and in control he was. Even when she'd shouted at him he hadn't lost his ice-cool composure.

'You don't like uncertainty?' He watched her steadily.

'I don't like being kept waiting.'

His eyebrows shot up. 'I'm taking the time to think.'

'Does it usually take you this long?' She didn't mean to be rude, but it surprised her. He was incredibly successful and she bet he hadn't become so by mulling over trivial decisions about low-level staff.

But wasn't she was doing him a disservice? He'd already stood up to those horrible, grasping relatives before she'd even arrived and he'd had no hesitation in showing them the door. She was finally about to offer a shamefaced, belated apology when he spoke.

'I've found that giving a problem my full consideration, rather than making a snap judgment, results in a better night's sleep for me.' He offered the slightest sarcastic curve to his lips in lieu of an actual smile.

She'd made a snap judgment that he was Harold's nephew, and this was an unsubtle rebuke for that. Yet it wasn't his reprimand that bothered her. It was another ripple of that forbidden feeling slithering down her spine. She did not need to be thinking about sleeping—specifically *him* sleeping—at this moment. And she did not need to be wondering what he'd look like with an actual, genuine smile on his face when he was already this attractive.

He studied her for another long moment and his gaze lowered to the resting creature in her arms. 'The dog is old,' he said bluntly.

'So that means we should just put him down?' she asked scornfully, her outrage torched again. The debate was on and she was fighting for Toby.

'He'll miss his owner,' Leon answered with surprising softness. 'He'll fret.'

The note of compassion from him oddly made her more uncomfortable.

'So we find him someone who can be with him all the time so he has the companionship he needs while he grieves.'

He reached out and petted the dog's head gently. Ettie froze, stunned by the illicit surge in her body at his closeness…the craving.

'He can't go to a shelter,' she added.

She couldn't help staring at Leon. She'd never seen someone as handsome, or as serious, and suddenly he felt more of a danger to her than when she'd thought him to be a heartless brute or when she'd thought he was going to fire her. The unaccustomed response within her to his fierce masculinity was shocking.

She whipped up her resistance. She didn't want to

like him. Of all the moments for her stagnant sensuality to spark up…

'Would you take him?' Curiosity burned in his eyes.

'I would,' she answered without hesitation. 'Except I'm at work all hours and he'd be lonely. And I'm not allowed pets in my building.'

'Pets aren't allowed in these apartments either,' he muttered. 'Isn't that the rule the previous owner implemented?'

'No resident ever minded Toby. He's lovely and he was around before that petty rule came into force.' She looked down at the dog protectively. She'd disliked that owner who'd wanted to charge more but offer less. He'd employed the awful George to enforce the 'new way'—most of which involved paying the staff less for more onerous rules and rosters, which had led to that festering resentment and feeling as if they couldn't be trusted. Ironically, the rumour was that the absent owner had got into money trouble… and now she was faced with this guy.

'You aided and abetted Mr Clarke in keeping Toby a secret, didn't you?'

They all had. But Ettie lifted her chin; she wasn't about to offer excuses or drag her friends under with her. 'Are you going to sack me for it?'

He remained impassive but she sensed his assessment. And his judgment. 'That depends. What other rules do you break?'

'Just the stupid ones.'

He watched, waiting for her to expand on her answer, but she refused. She was not going to desperately fill the awkward silence he was deliberately leaving. And she was not going to let his stunning looks have a stupefying effect on her brain any longer either. She was here for Toby—for the last thing she could do for old Harold Clarke.

'He needs to be in a familiar environment,' she said. 'Given he's not a nuisance to anyone, you should allow Toby to remain in Cavendish House, don't you think?' she asked with more defiance than deference in her voice.

Because more than anger bubbled within her at his silent appraisal and that stern stare beneath those slightly pulled strong eyebrows.

She tore her gaze from him and desperately looked around Harold's apartment to remind herself of her mission. The old man had been their longest resident. He'd mostly kept to himself, but he'd been kind and his dog had been his world. He'd protected the vulnerable even when he was vulnerable himself. 'We owe it to Harold to take care of Toby.'

'We?'

'Yes.' She lifted her chin pointedly and looked back at him. 'Why can't you take him?' she challenged directly.

There was another moment of total silence, but as she gazed into his eyes, the amber light within them flared. 'No reason that I can see,' he muttered.

She blinked. 'Pardon?'

'Toby will move to my penthouse. You'll take him for fresh air.'

Her jaw dropped. He wanted her to go to his penthouse? 'You want him to sleep in your apartment?'

'It's a temporary arrangement,' he said brusquely. 'On the condition that you walk him. You feed him. I do nothing but provide the space.'

The sizzle she felt was just her, right? She gave herself a mental shake. Just because he was insanely good-looking didn't mean she had to turn into a twittering ditz. She'd pull herself together and get the job done. 'You want me to—'

'Morning and night obviously. Yes.' He turned that cool demeanour on her and dared her to object.

Ettie was so stunned, she couldn't help questioning him. 'Why can't you walk him?'

The coldness that entered his expression now stunned her. 'We'll find a more permanent solution in a few days. In the meantime, there'll be no disturbance to the other residents.'

She was shocked. 'You really want me to—'

'Do I really need to repeat myself?'

'No. Of course not.' She stilled, annoyed with his superciliousness. Usually she'd say 'sir', but she was struggling to suppress her rebellion and tell this guy what for again. He couldn't walk or feed the dog himself? Was he for real?

And yet he'd just offered up his own space to ensure Toby's safety and security, so that the vulnerable little dog could stay.

What the hell had forced that foolish suggestion from him? Leon Kariakis smothered his growl and gritted his teeth. He didn't want anything to do with the dog. The ancient, arthritic creature was most probably incontinent and most definitely going to be a pain. Except he was a sweet-looking thing with the saddest eyes Leon had ever seen, and there was no way he could resist reaching out again to soothe the boy with a gentle pat. As he pulled back, he inadvertently brushed his fingers on Antoinette's arm. He glanced up to her face. Sea-green, luminous, emotion-drenched eyes glared back at him.

Why was she looking so angry again now?

He was the one who ought to be put out. And truthfully he was still oddly angered by her assumption he was the selfish bastard who'd issued the instruction to destroy the innocent creature. Somehow he wanted to make her pay for the conclusion she'd so swiftly, and unjustly, leapt to.

Not *somehow*.

His body knew *exactly* how he wanted her to pay. He wanted her to keep looking at him with those overly emotional green eyes, but not with anger and judgment. He wanted to see hunger and willingness. *Desire*.

Basic instinct roared. Because he knew it was there within her too. She'd studied him anew once she'd realised her error. And she'd responded on the same basic level as he had—the sparkle of awareness in her eyes, the flush in her face, had given her away.

He wanted her beneath and about him. His primal response to her passion shocked him. He wanted her in the most animal, basic of ways.

It was the most inappropriate thought of his life. Lusting after her was wrong. He was staying in the building for only a week or so to understand its processes first-hand before deciding on what changes needed to be made. The last thing he should do was flirt with one of the staff who was literally in his firing line. She was off-limits and he was never that out of control. Ever. This was a situation that required a swift conclusion. Yet he couldn't resist getting involved directly.

'You'll need to bring the dog and all his accoutrements.' He checked his watch and then glanced back at her.

'Yes, of course.' She lifted her chin.

The action didn't make her any taller. She remained a smidgeon shorter than the average woman and slight through the shoulders. Her dark blonde hair was swept off her face into a loose, messy ponytail and her wide green eyes offered unusually clear reflections of her feelings.

She wasn't the sleek automaton he'd envisaged when he'd been told about her. She wore barely any make-up—as far as he could tell, there was little more than a slick of lip gloss. Yet her skin was smooth, unblemished and glowing. The uniform black trousers and monogrammed T-shirt she wore did little to reveal much of her figure, but what they did show was slim and the suggestion of fit. His overall impression was of supple, fresh femininity. He'd been accosted by another of the more elderly residents in the lift this morning who'd been at pains to tell him that Antoinette Roberts was the only reason he'd remained at Cavendish House in recent years.

One look at her and Leon understood why.

But she wasn't his type. She'd spoken to him in a way no one else dared to. Tearing strips off him with blunt, brutal honesty, not stopping to censor herself or having the slightest hesitation in telling him what she really thought. Her heart wasn't just on her sleeve, she was waving it on a flag in front of him.

It was extremely novel. In his life, communicating emotions had not only been discouraged, but also punished. As his parents had ruthlessly taught him, any kind of emotional display was a weak loss of self-control.

Yet he didn't want Antoinette to start picking her words with care now. He liked knowing, without any uncertainty, exactly what she was feeling. And it was her fierce protectiveness that riveted him. Like a lioness protecting a lone cub, she'd held her corner and not given an inch, no matter the possible personal cost to herself. She'd fully expected him to fire her. But Leon knew people made mistakes. He'd give her one chance to redeem herself.

'Be on time. Always. I don't like to be disturbed,' he said roughly.

'I can be discreet,' she answered defiantly.

He simply stared at her. As if she could come into his apartment unseen? Unheard? As if she could ever be anything but disruptive?

A thread of wicked amusement trickled through him as she stilled in the face of his silence. He knew the exact moment she mentally replayed her words and realised an alternative innuendo. The same intimacy-drenched scenario he was imagining. A deep rose burnished her creamy skin—her cheeks, her neck, even the small hint of skin he could see at the vee of her high-collared T-shirt. But then he registered the rebellion in her gaze again—together with her less than subtle attempts to suppress it.

He didn't want her to suppress anything.

The urge to haul this petite emotional tornado close and kiss her into a frenzy of desire almost felled him. Grimly he fought the need to provoke her into taking everything else she might want from him. He knew he could. He saw the awareness in her eyes. Women found him attractive and sex was a fun relaxant. But he'd bet that sex with Girl Friday here wouldn't be as much fun as mind-blowing. If the incandescence of her anger was anything to go by, in bed she'd be unrestrained and utterly responsive.

Sex of the best kind. The kind that was irresistible.

He knew she felt the sparks. They were why she'd flushed over her choice of words. Why she'd trembled at his inadvertent touch before. Why she was looking at him with unrestrained rebellion now. Because she didn't want this chemistry either. And that irritating rejection was precisely why he couldn't resist making what he knew would be a massive mistake.

He roughly pushed the request past the tightness in his throat. 'I want you in my apartment in one hour.'

CHAPTER TWO

'Why didn't you tell me?' Ettie groaned to Joel as soon as she safely got back into the small concierge office, Toby still in her arms.

'I didn't have the chance…'

Of course he hadn't. Ettie shook her head and stopped him, regretting her unfair question. 'Sorry, I know you didn't.'

'Don't you think he's out of this world?' Jess, one of the housemaids, leaned over her desk. 'Chloe saw a model-type leaving his penthouse late last night. She was in the lift. Really dishevelled.' She waggled her eyebrows in a suggestive gesture. 'First night in and he's already—'

'No gossip,' Ettie whispered loudly, but softened her rebuke with a smile at the maid.

The news didn't surprise her. Of course he'd bed models. He was as striking as a model himself. He'd have no trouble getting any woman he wanted into bed. Even she'd responded to him on a purely primal level. He was so handsome it was almost painful. He was extraordinarily uptight, though, and he had a way of looking as if he could see right through her, while at the same time revealing nothing of his own thoughts.

Unabashed by Ettie's warning, Jess just laughed. 'Well, I think he's gorgeous. I'd do him.'

'He's an unsmiling ogre,' Joel grumbled. 'An arrogant jerk who thinks he's special.'

Well, with his obvious physical strength as well as his business success, he was a bit special. He had it all—looks, wealth, women…success.

'He was unfairly harsh with you, Ettie,' Joel added. 'And as for George…'

Yeah, it was no surprise that her boss was nowhere to be seen—hiding out until the dust had settled, no doubt. But she smiled at the hint of protectiveness in Joel's voice. 'He'll be even harsher if I don't get all that stuff up to his apartment within the hour.'

'Do you want help?'

She shook her head. 'We're behind down here already—you get on top of this for me and I'll deal with the ogre.'

She had to go into his apartment. Repeatedly. Her heart beat stupidly quickly at the thought. The range of inappropriate images that rioted through her head at the prospect of turning up to his apartment early tomorrow morning… Would he be awake or sleepy? She'd bet her life he didn't bother with pyjamas… but what if he had another dishevelled model-type with him? Ugh.

Get a grip and act like a professional.

Somehow she had less than fifteen minutes until the hour he'd given her was up, and she was not being late a second time today. With the dog in one arm and pushing a trolley with all his other stuff, she took the lift. She knocked but got no answer, so keyed in the security code.

'Hello? Mr Kariakis?' She walked into the apartment, but the room was silent.

Was she supposed to leave Toby alone in here or wait with him? Gritting back a frustrated sigh, she popped the dog down and turned to lift all his paraphernalia from the trolley. As she struggled with full arms, she noticed Toby wandering off towards a bedroom. She called to him quickly, dropping his water bowl as she hurried to catch him. And at that worst possible moment the ancient rubber band securing her ponytail snapped, sending her hair flying about her face in a mess of half-curls and straggle. She dumped the dog's gear down in the middle of the room and glanced about for something to use. She spied a pen lying on the nearest table and quickly swiped it up. She twisted her unruly hair into a knot on top of her head and secured it with the pen. Thank heavens perfect Leon Kariakis wasn't there to see her in such a debacle with the dog, basket, blankets and bowls all in a muddle at her feet.

'Ms Roberts.'

She froze. And wasn't that just her luck?

She swivelled to face him as he strode through from the bedroom. Usually it was at this point that she'd offer her first name to a new resident. Something held her back from doing so with Leon Kariakis, however. The grim look of disapproval on his face perhaps?

He still looked impeccable in that charcoal suit. She quelled the smidgeon of disappointment that he might've relaxed a little in his own space; it wasn't to be.

'You're late,' he said.

'Actually, I'm right on time.' She held up her watch and then walked further into the lounge, trying not to let her confidence plummet. Remote and controlled, he relentlessly watched her progress as she self-consciously set up Toby's basket in a corner of the room with a stunning view of the city out of the floor-to-ceiling windows.

'Is that my pen in your hair?'

She froze. Could his voice be any more arctic?

'Sorry, my hair tie broke.' She looked at him and registered the astonishment in his eyes. 'It's a special pen?'

'It can write upside down.'

Was he kidding? She couldn't contain an impish grin at his perennial solemnity. 'You do handstands and take notes?'

Was that an answering glint of humour in his eyes now?

'It's my pen.' He ignored her little joke. 'You stole it.'

'I *borrowed* it.' So much for any chance of a sexy librarian look with the whole hair-tied-in-a-bun thing. The man didn't soften an inch. She sighed. 'You'd like it back right away?'

'If you wouldn't mind.'

Seriously? He was that uptight about a *pen*?

As she took it out her hair tumbled into chaos. She was too aware of his gaze lingering on the unruly mess and then he returned to look at her eyes. Suddenly she felt hotter than when she'd been furious about what was going to happen to Toby.

She held the pen out to him. Wordlessly he took it and put it into the breast pocket of his jacket. Over his heart.

She quickly turned away, wishing he'd just leave her to it. Instead he watched the fall of her hair, and her every other move as she set out Toby's blanket and bowl. Toby padded straight into his basket and curled into a small ball.

Leon leaned against the wall, still watching intently as she gave the dog a couple of soothing pats.

'Is there nothing you can't do?' he asked.

She was unwilling but unable to resist looking up at him. She wasn't sure if he was being sarcastic or not, but she resolved to treat him as she did any other difficult client—with respect and *distance*.

'There's plenty I can't do,' she muttered softly. Keep her hair under control for one thing.

'You've thought of everything.'

She straightened. 'It's my job to think of everything.'

'And you're very good at your job,' he drawled.

She looked him directly in the eyes at that. 'Yes, I am.'

Which was why he wasn't going to sack her for

her earlier mistake. Which was why she was going to maintain a professional distance from him now.

Ophelia needed her to keep this job. She needed to remember that. She'd ignore the silent, magnetic pull.

'I assume Security has given you your own access code so it doesn't matter if I'm here or not.' His huskiness somehow built that sense of intimacy in the moment.

She nodded, momentarily fascinated by the discovery that his eyes weren't completely wintry; there were almost amber lights in them. Warm ones.

'This is a short-term solution,' he said. 'Until we can get him rehomed in a more suitable environment.'

'Of course.'

Focus, Ettie.

She looked around the room and then sent him a sideways look. 'Though this environment seems pretty suitable.'

Leon walked over to her and hunched down by Toby's basket. 'Is he always this subdued?' He patted the dog gently again. 'I wondered if he wasn't well.'

Ettie smiled at him, pleased he was concerned. 'He's old and quiet and missing Harold. He's probably wondering what on earth is going on...'

Leon absently scratched the dog's ears.

'His quality of life is good, though.' Ettie looked at him earnestly.

'Don't worry. I'm not about to summon the vet.'

For a split-second Ettie relaxed, but she was then hit by a flood of intense pleasure at seeing this powerful man almost kneeling at her feet. It was dizzying.

'I'll leave you two to get to know each other, then.' On an irresistible impulse, she teased him. 'Perhaps you could smile at him? Make him feel welcome?' That stupid suggestion had popped out before she'd thought better of it.

He suddenly stood. She'd not realised how near he was. Now he towered over her.

Don't prod a grumpy beast.

'Bare my teeth at him, you mean?' he muttered quietly. 'I'm not sure it's wise to do that to a wolf.'

That low pull tugged deep in her belly—purely physical, animal magnetism that set off a melting sensation deep within. Restless, inappropriate desire. With it came recklessness.

'One wolf to another?' she nudged dangerously. 'Don't you ever just smile?'

Oh, yes, she'd crossed a line now.

He didn't answer other than to stare down at her as if he couldn't believe what he'd heard. As if he was contemplating what kind of retribution he was about to mete out...

He liked to take the time to think, right?

Ettie had forgotten how to think. Or move. Or even breathe. She just stared right back at him for an endless moment. He really was far too handsome. And far too serious. She was utterly mesmerised. 'Thank you for taking care of him,' she whispered.

Something fierce flared in his eyes. 'Contrary to what you thought earlier, I'm not a monster.'

No, he wasn't. And she guessed he was allowed to be as serious as he liked, in his own home and all.

'I'm sorry for that mistake,' she finally apologised. Flushing with heat, she brushed a lock of her rebellious hair back from her face. Again.

He watched her movement as intently and inscrutably as ever. 'Thank you.'

She didn't feel forgiven, she felt flayed.

She didn't know if he stepped closer, or if she swayed, but suddenly there seemed to be no space at all between them. Her breath stalled in her lungs. He was so very close. But he was also utterly, inhumanly, still. He had such intensity of focus—expressionless, but not remote—and having that focus solely on her was more than dizzying, it was like being in the path of a lightning strike. She was going to get burned, but the chance to get lit up…?

Another long moment passed before her brain kicked back into operational mode. Oh, heaven, he probably thought she was waiting for him to make a move. He must get so many women throwing themselves at him. *Models* in the lift, remember? He'd never look twice at her. Mortified, she desperately clawed back her sanity and her dignity.

'I'd better get back downstairs,' she croaked, turned tail and fled.

Leon was hanging on to his control by the thinnest of threads. He'd spent the day determined to forget Antoinette Roberts. And for the first time in a very long time he'd spent a day failing.

She kept appearing in his thoughts—gorgeously fresh, her beautiful, wavy hair shimmering with every turn of her head. He never should have made her give his pen back because now he was beset with the fantasy of having that glorious hair spread across his pillows as the rest of her arched up to…

Leon stalked out of Cavendish House, his body aching. It was late in the evening but he'd not bother with dinner, he'd walk and wear himself out that way. Toby was fast asleep in his basket and too old to keep pace with him. He knew Antoinette had returned earlier to walk the dog and given him food. Leon had deliberately stayed away at the time, but the scent of her lingered in his rooms, sending his brain back into the direction he'd been trying to avoid all day.

Since when did he lose control over his own damn pulse? Ice-cool control was the one thing he always maintained. Antoinette Roberts threatened it with one fiery glance. Maybe it had been too long since he'd taken a lover. He should've taken up that offer last night.

Grimacing, he walked along the footpaths. The shops were open late and crowds milled about. He glanced sightlessly into the windows as he threaded through the masses. But through one immaculate window display he swore he recognised the gleaming rich hair of the petite woman standing with her back to him.

Great. Now he was seeing her everywhere.

But then he heard her voice as well—her lilting humour as she asked a customer if she needed help. He stared into the store, listening through the open door. Either Antoinette Roberts had a doppelgänger, or she'd come straight here after her shift at Cavendish and was now helping some woman choose a set of thank-you cards.

He walked in, quickly taking in the high-end stationery supplies the shop was stocked with. A couple of minutes later the female customer walked past him on her way out carrying a beautifully wrapped parcel and a satisfied smile on her face.

Leon walked up to the woman behind the counter. 'Ms Roberts?'

It was definitely her. And he definitely couldn't stop staring. Gone was the utilitarian, practical Cavendish concierge uniform and now she was in a lithe little black dress. He could finally see something of her legs and, just as he'd suspected, they were smooth, shapely and gorgeous. He'd known that if she could make those black trousers look sexy, she'd be dynamite in a dress. This one had a slightly scooped neckline, which meant there wasn't anywhere near enough cleavage, but there was skin—creamy, silken-looking skin and the suggestion of sweet curves beneath the fabric. And her glorious hair was freed from that bouncing mess of a ponytail and now cascaded in glossy wild waves down her back. It looked lush, as if it'd be soft to touch and he'd bind it around his wrists—

'Oh.' A blush flooded her smooth cheeks and she licked her lips. 'Mr Kariakis?' Then her wide-eyed gaze narrowed. 'You left Toby alone?'

The beseeching reproach in her eyes made him feel guilty even when he shouldn't. 'You know he ate a good dinner; now he's fast asleep. He's not missing me.'

The inward tension he'd been trying to settle tightened again. He'd needed to get out of that soulless apartment. He'd wanted to exorcise the ghost of her standing there, challenging him with that sassy look in her eyes as she'd flicked his stupid pen back at him. He'd been hopelessly distracted by the memory—but he was thrown back into that whirling web of desire again now.

'What are you doing here?' he asked irritably.

'What do you think I'm doing?' Her tone cooled to match his.

His tension spiked, he released it on her insane workload. 'You've worked all day already.'

She stiffened. 'Lots of people work more than one job. I'm sure you work long hours too.'

But there was a hint of tiredness in the backs of her eyes.

'You're tired.' He refused to believe she wanted to work fourteen or more hours a day.

'Oh, no,' she answered airily. 'Actually as soon as I'm done here, I'm going clubbing.'

'Are you?' He fired with her challenge. 'Excellent. Take me with you—I'm new to town and don't know all the cool places.'

A disconcerted expression crossed her face and he inwardly laughed. He couldn't lie to himself any more. His offer to care for the dog was based in selfish motivation: to see more of Antoinette. He wanted her in his bed. Ideally tonight. It had hit in that first second—lust at first sight. Lust that was only increasing the longer he spent in her company. Perhaps if he satisfied the urge, it'd disappear as swiftly as it had come.

And her reaction to him? He could tempt her.

'I…' She glanced at her watch and that flush across her delicate, high cheekbones built.

It was five minutes until closing and he wasn't planning on leaving. 'You like working here?'

He made conversation to ease her embarrassment. Despite those delicious feisty flashes, she displayed hints of shyness. He found the combination unbelievably tantalising.

'It's nice.' She nodded.

He tensed. 'Nicer than Cavendish?'

Was she thinking of leaving her concierge job? In some ways that would be good—it would free them of any messiness, given their positions there.

'It's quieter than Cavendish, but I don't build the same relationship with my customers as I do there. I only work the late nights here.' She glanced at the counter display. 'It's beautiful stationery.'

'That's why you work here—because you like the product?'

A bubble of laughter burst from her shimmering lips. 'No, if I just liked the product, I'd buy it.'

'So it's money.' He frowned, unhappy at the thought that she was forced to work two jobs. 'We don't pay you enough.'

A wary expression crossed her face. 'It's fine. I have commitments. Most of us do, right?'

He shouldn't pry further but he couldn't help watching intently, waiting to see if she'd say more. Her clear eyes dimmed with faint shadows.

'Saving,' she muttered, unable to help herself.

Unusually for him, his curiosity deepened. But it wasn't his business. He had no right to press further. 'Good for you.'

She nodded awkwardly. 'So did you want anything in particular?'

He bit back the blunt answer of what he particularly *wanted* and made himself breathe first. 'I wanted to see if it was really you.'

'Well.' That impish smile flashed on her lips, flicking away the shadows in her eyes. 'It is.'

'In another uniform.' He couldn't help noticing that damned demure neckline again.

'Black again.' She bit her lip as she quickly glanced down as if afraid she'd spilled something. 'Always ready for a funeral, that's me,' she quipped. 'But it's discreet. Unobtrusive.'

'I would never describe you as unobtrusive,' he muttered quietly.

She'd burst into his life in a blaze of passion and fury.

She met his gaze, silently questioning just how he'd describe her. Unspoken awareness flickered between them, like a gravitational pull.

Her blush returned full force, a ruby tide over her creamy complexion. 'I should get back to work. It's almost time to close.'

She was flustered again. He was fascinated by her

unconscious dance—she advanced closer with those challenges, then retreated in shyness. He glanced around the shop, pleased to discover it had emptied completely of other customers. 'Show me the biggest seller.'

'Seriously?' The droll scepticism on her face was a picture.

Entertained by her expressiveness, he leaned closer. 'Why not? You don't think I can afford it?'

She sent him another look. 'Well, I know you don't need a new *pen*.' She lifted an item from the counter and met his gaze with a prim, shop-girl pose. 'But we have an exquisite range of journals.'

'Exquisite,' he echoed dryly.

'Incredibly so,' she emphasised, refusing to acknowledge his soft sarcasm.

'What is it about girls and diaries?' He reached out and traced the smooth leather cover with his finger. 'Do you pour out your soul into one of these every night?'

'What if I do?' She lifted her chin in that irresistibly defiant gesture.

'Would it make for fascinating reading?' He was appallingly curious now. For the first time intrigued enough to want to know all a woman's thoughts, all her wishes, every last secret and deepest desire.

'Sadly, no. I only keep lists in mine.' She reached across the counter and flipped an open book around to show him. 'See?'

'This is yours?' His pulse rate lifted.

'I work on it in quiet moments,' she said. 'I have

permission from my boss—it's good to see our products in use.'

Her defensiveness amused him. Was she as discomforted by him as much as he was by her? He leaned closer to read the scrawled list.

'I forget things,' she added nervously. 'I'm naturally disorganised, so I work hard to get it together and nail my job. Lists are the only thing that work for me.' She tried to pull the journal back but he planted his hand down to keep it there. His fingers brushed against her for the second time that day. Skin touched skin. She stilled, as did he.

A millisecond later she snatched her hand back. But he knew she'd felt that current of electricity flow between them.

He turned the pages of her journal, refusing to feel any remorse—she was the one who'd offered it for his viewing. But to his disappointment there were no deepest desires on show inside. Only ruthless organisation, as she'd said.

'Everything in your life is dictated by a list?' There were reminders, shopping lists, ticked-off tasks, pros and cons for other things... 'It's a lot of lists.' He flicked through more pages, wishing there were something far more personal in it. 'And in a rainbow of colours.'

'It doesn't need to be boring. Right? But I'm no artist, so I just choose a different colour for each...'

'I have a planner,' he offered idly. 'But it's online.'

'Online?' She shuddered theatrically. 'I couldn't

get all these lists on the one screen. And what if it got deleted?'

'What if you lost your journal?' he countered with the obvious. 'What if someone you don't want to read it gets hold of it?'

Her impish grin darted back. 'That's why there are only lists and reminders.'

'So, nothing too personal or incriminating?' He sighed with genuine disappointment. 'You're not a risk-taker, then.'

Her eyes widened.

'You won't run the risk of someone discovering your secrets,' he explained.

'Perhaps I don't have any,' she muttered.

'Everyone has secrets.' *And desires.*

Silent, she just gazed back at him.

'And I'll bet you're not really going clubbing,' he added quietly.

This time her smile was more sheepish than impish, and she shook her head.

'Have you had dinner?' He didn't give her time to answer. 'I don't think you've had time if you came straight from your shift at Cavendish. You must be hungry.'

He saw her hesitate and spoke again before she could deny it. 'Have dinner with me.'

'No thanks,' she instantly answered.

'Am I that awful?' he shot back, unafraid to challenge her directly. He knew what he wanted. He knew what she wanted too. He was just more honest about it.

She stared at him for a moment, shocked. 'No, I—'

'Well, don't let me down so roughly. It's only dinner.'

Roughly? Ettie narrowed her eyes on him. He was pulling her leg, right? Behind that serious facade there was some humour. 'It's not a wise idea. You're my boss.'

'It's not a date, just dinner. If it makes you feel better, you can tell me about life on the concierge desk. I need to know how the whole operation works. There'll be no repercussions for complete honesty.' He paused. 'Anyway, I'm not really your boss.'

Yeah, right. 'You own the building I work in.'

'But a management company employs the staff.'

'Do you own the management company?' She wouldn't have been surprised if he did.

'They're contracted... I don't own them.'

'So that makes it okay?' Her heart was pounding unnaturally fast.

'I think it creates a technicality we can take advantage of.' He looked right at her. Those amber flecks in his eyes lit up with every word. 'And you like breaking the stupid rules, right? This is a stupid one. Besides, I'm only living in the penthouse while I get my head around the building. Then I'll lease it to a client and move to my next investment, so you won't see me much.'

His message couldn't be clearer. He was saying he'd stay out of her way. That his presence was temporary. That this was just dinner. Just one night.

But Ettie needed a moment.

'You don't ever want to stay in one of your buildings?' She was intrigued by his transitory lifestyle.

'I like projects. I like the excitement and unique challenge of each one, and once I've overcome that challenge it's time to move on to another.'

She suspected he wasn't just talking building acquisition. It was lovers as well. 'You get bored easily?'

A speculative gleam heated his eyes even more. Yeah, he was talking on more than one level. But he answered with that customary seriousness. 'I like to keep busy. I like having problems to grapple with.'

'You don't ever want to just blob out on the beach?'

He cocked his head and considered it briefly. 'It's not something I've ever done.'

'Seriously?' She frowned. 'Not ever?' Didn't his parents own all those hotels in Greece? Wasn't that the ultimate holiday destination? 'You never have holidays?'

'Do you?' he countered.

'I don't have much choice.' She grimaced. 'I work hard but I don't have the same financial rewards, and I have obligations...' Which she didn't want to go into with him right now. 'What's the point in all your success if you don't stop and celebrate it every so often?'

'The point is the success itself,' he answered.

'You don't get tired?' She was flummoxed. If she could take a break somewhere warm and beautiful, she'd be there in a heartbeat.

'Don't worry,' he murmured. 'I know how to relax.'

Yeah, she bet he did. She sent him a reproachful glare and he suddenly laughed. Ettie gaped, stunned at his instant transformation from unsmiling auto-crat to hot, buttered hunk. She dragged oxygen into her tight lungs. It wasn't right that a man should be *so* gorgeous.

'It's not what you're thinking,' he said. 'Well, not entirely.'

'How do you know what I'm thinking?'

'It's written all over your face.'

Hopefully not *everything* she was thinking. And hopefully it wasn't obvious how her innards were positively melting. 'So you don't do this often? Pick up women and take them to dinner?'

'No, not often, actually. Does that surprise you?' His expression returned to serious as he studied her. 'You don't believe me?'

'You've been seen with other women,' she said.

His eyebrows shot up. 'When?'

'Last night, apparently.' She tried to play it cool but she was already regretting bringing it up. 'A woman leaving your apartment.'

He'd probably been celebrating his first night in Cavendish House.

Now Leon studied her for another long moment. She knew he was thinking. She just wished she knew *what*.

'You were talking about me.' His lips curved ever so slightly. 'You were curious.'

Before she had the chance to deny it, or to apol-ogise, or to melt in a swelter of embarrassment, he continued softly.

'Was she seen in my company?' he asked. 'I don't

think so. The woman who left my apartment late last night had arrived only minutes earlier. She's an acquaintance who'd heard I'd moved in. She came to see me as a surprise but it wasn't something I wished to pursue.'

'You don't like surprises like that?'

What red-blooded man wouldn't want to be surprised by some model-type turning up at midnight with a booty call on her mind?

'I already told you,' he replied. 'I like challenges.'

Surely he didn't see *her* as a challenge?

But she was pleased somehow, that he didn't dally with anyone and everyone who offered.

Leon picked up her journal from the counter and opened it again to look at the long columns of her lists. 'You could write a list about whether or not to have dinner with me.' He shook his head and snapped her book shut. 'Or you could just trust your instincts.'

Ettie regarded him warily. Her very basic instincts were hell-bent on leading her into trouble and her instincts had let her down before. Leon Kariakis was pure temptation and he knew it. Unfortunately for him, she was determined to remain in control of herself.

But this was a dare and he didn't scare her.

'All right, then,' she decided with spirit. 'Only to tell you all about the Cavendish.'

'Wonderful.'

He waited while she closed up the shop and set the security alarm. She grabbed her coat, but despite the chill in the air she didn't put it on. The thing was ancient and the zip was broken and she didn't want him seeing how worn it was.

'What do you usually have for dinner?' he asked as they walked along the crowded footpath.

Usually on the nights she'd worked late she grabbed a chocolate bar from the tube station on the way home or didn't bother. Tonight had been going to be a not-bother night. But she wasn't about to admit that. 'I might cook a quick stir-fry.'

'But if you were to dine out?'

She shrugged as nonchalantly as possible. Truth? She *never* dined out.

He sent her a sideways look. 'I know a good place.'

'I thought you were new to the area and didn't know any of the cool places.' She couldn't help smiling.

'I asked one of the concierges at my apartment building,' he replied smoothly. 'They offer a superb service.'

She rolled her eyes and kept pace with him along the busy footpath. A couple of corners later he paused outside a beautiful brick mansion.

She shook her head at him. 'No chance. You have to have a booking.'

He shrugged as if he wasn't fazed. 'We won't take up much space.'

It was a celebrity chef's place—the kind you had to make a reservation for six months in advance, which was actually a good thing, as it then gave you the time to save the small fortune you needed just to enjoy an appetiser, let alone sample the full menu. Ettie made bookings all the time on behalf of her Cavendish residents.

But Leon simply walked up to the door, which the discreet security guard immediately opened. The maître d' swept towards them, his wide gaze fixed firmly on Leon and his smile welcoming and wide. Leon didn't even need to utter a word.

'May I have five minutes, sir, if you'd like a drink first?'

'Thank you,' Leon answered with the ease of one born to privilege. 'Champagne?' He turned to Ettie.

'Lemonade,' she replied firmly and caught a gleam of pure amusement in his eyes.

'Definitely not a risk-taker,' he murmured.

'Fine, then,' she breathed. 'Champagne.'

One glass wouldn't do any harm.

They'd barely been given their drinks when the maître d' reappeared to lead them through the busy dining room. Ettie tried not to stare. Several faces were familiar to her but not through personal acquaintance. These were publicly led lives—an actress, a politician. Possibly a minor royal? They stopped at a secluded table in an alcove near the rear of the restaurant. It was quieter than the main dining room, more intimate and far more private.

'You like it?' Leon asked as she took her seat.

'You know the owner?' She hazarded a guess as she tried not to stare at the gleaming lighting and sumptuous décor, but she couldn't hold back her smile. The place was amazing. 'This is really kind of you.'

'No, I'm not really kind,' he corrected bluntly. 'This is pure self-interest. I get a pretty companion for dinner to take my mind off my misery.'

'Misery?' She quirked an eyebrow while battling the warmth she felt at his compliment. He didn't really mean it. He was just adding 'charming' to his repertoire, which was very unfair of him. 'Because your life's so terrible?' Curious, she watched him keenly for his answer.

But he turned the conversation back on her. 'Was it really going to be a stir-fry?'

'No,' she admitted with a chuckle. 'I hate cooking. Generally I exist on grilled cheese sandwiches.'

'There's a place in the world for a good grilled cheese sandwich.' He nodded. 'But not here.'

'Then what do you suggest?'

'I suggest we leave it to the experts.' He nodded at the maître d', who, with a slight bow, left for the kitchen. 'So, why are you working such intense hours?' Leon sipped his champagne. 'Do we not pay you enough to live on?'

She too took a sip and savoured the fizz of bubbles before replying. 'I'm saving.'

'For travel? A house?'

She laughed and shook her head. Was she really here to *entertain* him and take his mind off whatever torments he thought he had? 'I've a younger sister who aspires to go to university.'

'It's just the two of you?'

She nodded and took another sip.

'How old is she?' His gaze narrowed.

'Seventeen. She's away at boarding school up north.'

'You support her financially?'

'She's on a partial scholarship.'

'And you pay the rest?' His mouth tightened. 'But you're not that far out of school yourself.'

'I'm twenty-three, so a few years out. It's her last year, so it really counts.'

'And she's obviously talented.'

'Top of her school.' Ettie beamed with unashamed pride. 'She's amazing. She wants to study medicine. So.' She inhaled deeply. 'A lot of study.' And a lot of tuition and living fees. But Ophelia was worth it and she'd do anything to see her achieve her dreams.

'What happened to your parents?'

'Twenty questions, huh?' She sent him a look but answered anyway. 'My father was never around. My mother passed away a couple of years ago.'

'That must have been hard.'

It had been but she didn't want to dwell on her mother's slow decline with cancer. Not tonight. Not here. She smiled softly. 'We've survived.'

She didn't tell him about the huge mistake that she'd made not long after her mother's death either. The total car crash that had been her love life.

'What's your sister's name?'

'Ophelia.'

'Antoinette and Ophelia,' he said quietly. 'But you're "Ettie"?'

'Yes, fingers crossed neither of us suffers the delusions or disappointment of our namesakes.' She sat back as the waiter appeared and placed dishes on the table. 'My mother was a romantic.' Not that she'd had any kind of romantic luck. Like mother, like daughter. 'This looks amazing.'

She was pleased to have the interruption to the topic. And she realised she was absolutely *starving*.

He waited for her to take a bite, amusement softening his innate seriousness. 'What do you think? Better than a grilled cheese sandwich?'

Ettie couldn't answer, she was too busy salivating. But she finally swallowed her mouthful. 'I've never eaten anything like it. It's to die for.'

And that was all she could say, because she needed more this instant. He probably thought she was an idiot, but right this second she didn't care. This was one of those rare experiences in life that had to be luxuriated in.

'Here, try this.' He pushed another plate towards her.

Ettie tasted what was, frankly, the food of the gods. Conversation turned to flavours and textures. Leon was animated, knowledgeable and entertaining as they debated which dish was the most delicious.

'Do you have room for dessert?' he teased her almost an hour later as she sat back with a satisfied sigh.

'I should say no, because I'm not remotely hungry now…' She trailed off.

When was she ever going to be in a restaurant like this again? With a man like this? It was a once-in-a-lifetime fantasy night and she didn't want it to end.

'What if we share?' He offered her pure temptation.

She flashed a huge grin at him. 'I get to pick, right?' she said impulsively. 'Because you can come here any time.'

He laughed a little beneath his breath. 'Sure.'

'Or maybe you should pick.' She suddenly back-pedalled, remembering the guy was all but her boss. 'You probably know what's good...'

There was a quizzical light in his eye and his eyebrows twitched. 'I'm sure they're all good.' He turned and said something softly to the waiter who'd magically appeared with his impeccable service-required senses on full alert.

Ettie narrowed her gaze on Leon. 'You did not just order every dessert on the menu.'

'You don't have to eat them all, just taste.'

Her jaw dropped at the decadence of the suggestion and she shook her head. 'That's wasteful.'

'Then we can take the rest home for later,' he said softly.

Ettie stilled, swamped with heat at the suggestion of intimacy that throwaway comment inferred. Was he assuming she'd go home with him tonight?

Images burned in her brain—of her licking a decadent chocolate dessert while in bed with him. Even better, licking said chocolate dessert *off* him.

'Ettie?' He was watching her closely as if he could read her mind. 'You can take them home and have them for breakfast,' he clarified in a slightly husky voice.

The less than subtle undercurrents between them

were unbearably strong and gaining power with every passing second. She licked her suddenly dry lips and decided it was his turn to answer twenty questions. 'Do you have any brothers or sisters?'

He hesitated and for a moment she thought he wasn't going to answer.

But his mouth twisted. 'I'm an only child. Spoilt little rich boy.' His tone was mocking, but the edge of bitterness ran deeper than a mere joke.

'But you built your own business, right?' She knew his parents had that Greek hotel empire, but he'd gone into finance on his own. That was according to the official bio in his 'most eligible bachelor' blurb in the magazine Jess the housemaid had been flashing around this afternoon at work.

He shook his head. 'I had every advantage—education, health, wealthy parents. While my business success is my own, I can't rightly claim to have done it all by myself when I came from that starting point. Most people don't get that privilege to begin with.'

'But you made the most of your opportunities.'

Of course those schools, those contacts—sure they helped. But in the end, he had to do the work himself. And there were plenty of heirs to vast fortunes who'd frittered their lives away.

A lick of something indefinable flickered in his eyes. 'I like to extract every possible success from every possible scenario. Yes.'

Again that undercurrent swept over her like a blanket of wild dizziness—sensuality of a kind she'd never encountered or imagined. Sexual tension so intense…but it was also teasing, almost fun. Which was surprising, given he was so very serious…and she so very inept at banter.

Two waiters appeared and set six dishes on the table. Six decadent desserts that were miniature works of culinary art.

'They're only small portions,' she said softly, as if that made it better. 'I imagine they're rich.'

'Why don't you take a bite and find out?' That tone was back—dry on the surface, but wicked beneath—daring her to take the risk, to take a bite of something so far out of her league. To taste something miles away from her realm of experience.

She picked up the silver fork and forced herself to focus on the glorious-looking *food*, rather than the man across the table mesmerising her. She took a moment to mentally debate which she should taste first—it was a three-way contest between the chocolate nirvana, the caramel or the raspberry heaven. In the end the chocolate won.

Ettie closed her eyes as she sucked the rich mousse from the spoon.

'Good?'

It was impossible to answer him—the deliciousness too much to express. It was like all the good things in the world had been put together in the one flavour bomb and it had just burst on her tongue.

'Have you tried this?' she mumbled with her mouth full. 'Because I'm not sure I can share after all. And there aren't going to be any leftovers, sorry.'

Leon covered his mouth but she could see deep laughter dancing in his eyes.

'Don't hide your smile,' she scolded recklessly,

cross with him for hiding that spark from her. She just knew that had been a gorgeous smile and she wanted to bask in the full impact of it.

'You have great teeth,' she added dizzily as she swallowed more of the silken chocolate. 'Are you afraid I might think you're human? Because don't worry, we all know you're…' She trailed off, suddenly aware she shouldn't complete that rambling sentence.

'I didn't want you to think I was laughing at you,' he said with mock-defensiveness. 'Some women get sensitive about being seen enjoying food.'

Who? Those model-types he hung out with?

'I'm not bothered,' she said honestly. 'I'm utterly unashamed about enjoying this…' She breathed out and surveyed the luscious desserts still before her.

'Well, *I'm* the one offended,' he muttered. 'You don't think I'm human?'

Hmm, unfortunately she had said that. 'I also said you have great teeth.' Which was even more mortifying, but she smiled at him anyway.

'All the better to bite you with,' he answered severely, but she saw the sparkle in those amber-lit eyes of his. No, he wasn't anywhere near as serious as she'd first thought. He was *guarded*. So guarded he'd been wary of letting her see him relax. Why was he so defensive when he had everything?

'Perhaps I deserve a bite,' she acknowledged with a chuckle. 'But you were laughing at me.'

His expression turned sly. 'So are you offended?'

'I'm not that precious. You suit a smile. You should do it more often. If I lived in Cavendish House I'd be smiling all the time.' And if she owned the place, she'd be doing back-flips.

'It's not bricks and mortar that make people happy.'

'Oh, they help.' She laughed openly at that. 'Here, taste this. It'll help too.'

'Oh, am I allowed some now?' Sending her a speaking look, he picked up his fork.

Ettie's pulse skidded all over the place as Leon escorted her out of the restaurant. She shrugged on her coat just for something to do and turned, ready to walk to the train station. She refused to let her spirits lower now the night was over.

He caught her hand in his. Electricity surged at the firm clasp of his fingers over hers and a new level of intimacy seared. She knew it had been building between them, yet she was suddenly shy, but overwhelmingly she wanted everything she probably shouldn't.

He turned her to face him.

'So, clubbing?' he asked.

She couldn't seem to speak, so she just shook her head.

'You don't want to dance with me?' he asked quietly.

Oh, she wanted to dance with him. Just the two of them. Intuitively she knew he was asking for just that—an *intimate* dance. It was fantastic. But ever since he'd walked into the stationery shop, it was as though she'd stepped into another dimension—an alternative reality where the truths of tomorrow really didn't matter and where the past was irrelevant and where for one crazy night this way-out-of-her-league guy was paying her attention.

He stepped closer, his expression intensifying— even more serious, and *hungry*.

'This is a very bad idea,' he said softly.

'Yes,' she agreed softly. She couldn't quite believe he even wanted to get closer to her, but here he was, leaning in with so much intent.

She'd been working so hard for so long. She'd been let down too many times. She'd been alone for what felt like for ever. What did it matter if there was no future in this? She'd pinned her hopes on a future with a man before, only to be heartbroken. With no hopes, no expectations…there would be no heartbreak, right?

'Terrible.' He lifted his hand and gently framed her face.

She quivered at that lightest of touches. 'Yes.'

She read the sultry promise in his eyes as those pros and cons swirled in her head. What was the worst that could happen? She'd have an amazing experience with a god-like man. And whether he enjoyed it as much as she…well, that was up to him, wasn't it? Couldn't she let that fear go?

'But I want to do it anyway.'

He did? He really did? She smiled and her tummy swarmed with butterflies…but below that, molten heat swirled. 'Yes.'

There was only now. Only this sensation. Only this one chance. And she wanted it.

'And so do you?' His gaze searched hers intently.
'Yes.' *Of course.*

She might be inexperienced, but she wasn't stupid.

'And that's all you're going to say tonight?' His lips twitched.

She stared at him, willing him to smile. 'Yes.'

'To anything I ask?'

She'd not taken a moment purely for herself in such a long time. 'Um…yes.'

His mouth didn't curve into a smile; instead it moved closer. He brushed a light kiss on her lips. Ettie remained still, her face upturned to his, not quite sure this was actually happening. He too was immobile, watching her with that ultra-serious, inscrutable intensity. She didn't want him to watch, she wanted him to *act*.

And then he did.

He cupped her head, threading his fingers through her hair to draw her closer so he could kiss her properly. Not a gentle brush of the lips, but a devastating, can't-get-enough kiss that mirrored the desire clawing deep in her body. That deliciousness in the restaurant was nothing on the sensations shivering through her body now. He devoured her as if she were the best of all those award-winning desserts. She lost track of time and place, there was no more thought, no more doubt as sensation transcended—and overwhelmed— everything. There was only one destination for her tonight and that was right here in his arms, with his mouth sealed on hers and his lips, hands, tongue and heat all working that dizzying magic. He made her tremble, made her want more than she'd ever wanted *anything*.

She moaned, totally overcome. 'Leon—'

He stepped back so suddenly she nearly stumbled. He quickly clamped an arm about her but somehow walked her forward at the same time. He waved and hailed a taxi. Of course one pulled over immediately—he had that way about him. People instantly recognised power, influence, money, and moved the minute he asked.

He thrust a couple of large notes to the driver through the window. 'Just drive.'

He hustled her into the cab ahead of him, then joined her on the back seat and pulled her in as if he'd been starved of kisses for aeons and was now making up for it. A famished, demanding man now feasting. She was okay with that. So okay. Because she'd discovered her own hunger—her own pleasure in exploring him too. She ran light fingers along his jaw, feeling that hot, sexy stubble—still unable to believe that she was really touching him and he was touching her. She was suddenly super-hot, although neediness made her shiver.

His hand skated over the hem of her dress. His teasing fingers circled, finding bare skin, seeking out more. Ettie quivered but he kept kissing her, and excitement thrummed throughout her body. Who knew kissing could be this erotic? This intense? This incredibly awesome?

She never wanted it to end. Time needed to stop. Because this was *it*. This was her moment—just for her. And he knew—he kept kissing her, increasing the dizzying intensity and turning up the heat with every luscious lick and slide. His teasing fingers skimmed her thigh so lightly it was only a slight tickle. Yet powerful waves of heat rolled over her. Her mouth parted more as she moaned and lifted her hips to quicker meet the delicious, unpredictable stroke of his fingertips. The tease was intolerable. She wanted a firmer touch. She wanted *more*.

He deepened the kiss further still, his tongue wickedly caressing inside her mouth until she was dizzy on the delight of it. He'd unleashed a hunger, a driving need she'd never known. She soared on the sensation, strung higher with that exquisite tension he drew her along with. She couldn't stop the rock of her hips now, instinctively enticing him to touch further, touch harder. His teeth nipped her lower lip just as he skimmed his fingertips higher—all the way to her soft, simple cotton panties. She gasped at the caress. He stilled and lifted his lips a mere millimetre from hers. Then those trespassing fingers stroked once more—so intimately that she violently squirmed, unable to hold back a moan as her fingers curled into fists. *Yes.* That was what she wanted. But he suddenly broke the kiss. Breathlessly she stared up at him. His gaze ensnared hers—his eyes were dark with promise, with satisfaction, with *hunger*.

He growled the address for Cavendish House to the taxi driver, their gazes still locked. Dazed, she read the determination in his eyes, felt the possessiveness of his hand cupping her so intimately, and understood exactly. He wanted *everything*.

If she was going to stop this, to say no, the time to do it was now. But it was also the time to say yes. Was she really going to be another of Leon Kariakis's conquests? His challenge for the night?

Yes.

Now she was in this other world of touch and light and scorching sensation, nothing could stop her from having this. Having him.

Just once.

She'd worked hard to rein in her natural impulsiveness. She'd had too much responsibility to be reckless...but this was only one night.

'Yes?' he prompted in a gruff undertone.

She nodded. She wanted the experience she knew he could give her. He swooped and kissed her again—pure reward, pure promise, invoking that breathless restlessness all over again. But he slipped his hand from beneath her dress and rested it on her breast instead, almost holding her captive. She acquiesced to everything, to the kiss, to the utterly foregone conclusion of this night—and simply drowned in the flood of pleasure his exquisite passion pulled from her.

But as they neared the building she suddenly clutched his wrist and whispered with panic, 'No one can see me.'

'In my company?' He half laughed at her drama and discomfort. 'I've already thought of that, don't worry.' He leaned forward and spoke to the taxi driver again. Moments later the gate to the underground garage slid open, letting them escape the cab unseen.

In the lift Leon pushed a series of buttons on the security pad. 'The lift will go straight to the penthouse. It won't stop on any other floor.'

Even so, she stood as far from him as possible because there was still a security camera in there. She wasn't ashamed but she was protective of her privacy and she didn't want her colleagues knowing that she'd... Embarrassed warmth flooded her and she fixed her gaze to the floor and let her hair fall forward, hoping her face couldn't be seen. At the ding of the bell, the doors slid open to his penthouse suite.

Leon led the way, keeping a little distance as he swiftly shrugged off his jacket and tie and tossed them onto the nearest sofa. 'Toby's asleep,' he said easily.

Ettie took the moment to pause and settle her heartrate. The elderly dog was comfortably curled in his basket and she could see he'd drunk some of his water. She breathed out a little of her tension as she glanced back at Leon. 'Why'd you take him?'

'Same reason you would have if you could,' he answered. 'Why did it surprise you so much that I did? Why think I'm such an ogre?'

Was there a hint of hurt in his eyes?

'I don't think you're an ogre,' she said softly. 'You can just come across as a bit stern.'

'You want me to smile?' He sounded sardonic.

'Yes.'

But he remained as still and as serious as ever. 'Come here.'

His request—command really—was impossible to ignore. She was drawn to him; she had been from the first moment she'd seen him. So she went to him, her heart thundering faster with every step.

'You're sure about this, Ettie?' he asked.

'Just this once,' she whispered. 'Only this once, okay?'

Leon didn't reply. He was so very still, so very serious. She knew he was thinking, she just didn't know what. But she sensed his tension, some kind of warring within. Instinctively she reached out and placed her hand on his chest.

His heart echoed hers—beating with a fierce gallop. The pace reverberated through her palm, up her arm and into her own tightly wired body. His enigmatic gaze glittered down at her.

And then he smiled.

CHAPTER THREE

ETTIE BLINKED, STUNNED again by his instant transformation from moody male model to sinfully arrogant tease. Oh, she was in such trouble. 'What are you thinking about?'

'The best way to begin.'

She swallowed as her poor heart raced even more. But lower down she melted with anticipation. 'Did you need some help with that?' she asked weakly. 'Should we list the options?'

He laughed, which made him all the more heart-stoppingly handsome. But just as she gaped—beyond dazzled—he swooped. He caught her gasp in his kiss, sending Ettie straight back into that intense desire she'd felt in the taxi. Oh, the man could *kiss*. He was playful and teasing—alternating deep, luscious licks with light nibbles that were designed to provoke her to madness. She had more freedom now than in the car, so she wound her arms around his neck and pushed closer, revelling in the press of his hard, masculine body against hers. He was tall and taut and she felt the strength in his core stillness. But his wicked hands wandered again, back to the hem of her dress, back to the silky skin of her inner thigh. She moaned, collapsing against him and letting her feet slide further apart as he trailed those fingertips to the top of her leg, teasing so, so close to where she ached to be teased.

Oh, yes. Please, yes.

But she didn't say it, didn't chant the plea circling in her head. She couldn't—she was too busy being kissed to glorious dizziness. But he must have read her mind, because then he went there—skilfully circling that tight bundle of pure sensitivity. She gasped, breaking the seal of the kiss as pleasure rushed upon her.

'*Oh...*'

He clamped her to him with his other arm, supporting her as the orgasm sent her body into spasms of blissful sensation. Never had she come so quickly with a man. Well, never had she actually *come* with a man.

Panting and suddenly so self-conscious, she pressed her forehead against his chest. He stroked her back but kept that other hand gently cupping her so intimately, soft touches easing her down yet keeping her hyper-aware of him.

'I've been imagining that all day,' he muttered low in her ear.

Really? Breathlessly she laughed as he suddenly switched his hold and lifted her off her feet to carry her through to the master bedroom.

'Me too,' she muttered shyly as he lowered her to stand at the foot of the big bed. So much.

His smile flashed again and it was like being concussed—all circling stars and dizziness, and she really didn't think she could stand for too much longer. She didn't think she could ever get enough of those smiles. But he stepped close and her eyes drifted shut as he kissed her all over again. Vaguely she heard the slide of her zip and before she realised it her dress had slithered to the floor in a sleek heap at her feet.

'Multitasking?' she mumbled in a moment of embarrassment at the simplicity of her exposed underwear. It was black, cotton—no lace or fancy silk and nothing like what any of those models would wear.

But he was still and staring again, erotic hunger stark upon his face. 'You're even more gorgeous than I imagined.'

She crossed her arms and shook her head.

He smiled again but there was an edge of craving to it. 'You don't believe me?' He stepped forward. 'Never mind.' He caught her in a kiss again and then pushed her so she fell back onto the bed. He moved onto the bed too, braced above her, kissing not just her yearning mouth but also down her neck and then lower still. She wriggled but he put a firm hand on her.

'Let me,' he ordered with a low mutter. 'I've wanted to for hours.'

He removed her bra with the skill of a man who'd undone many women. Frankly Ettie was glad as he then kissed his way from one breast to the other, teasing each nipple to a stiff peak of yearning. She quivered as he trailed teasing hands down her ribs to her hips. What was she supposed to do? How could she possibly resist? Her legs had a will of their own and simply spread—earning her a burning glance and then another of those soul-searing smiles. And then he put those lips to even better use.

'*Oh, my, oh, my, oh, my.*' This time she muttered the chant over and over as he teased her. As those hands pulled the panties from her body and his fingers sought out even more secrets. He was kissing her where no one had bothered to kiss her before. It was so shockingly intimate. So incredibly good.

'Leon,' she moaned, half drawing her knees up in rejection as his tongue swirled to even greater intimacy.

She felt the hot breath of his laughter. It tickled and she wriggled a little—half escaping, a whole lot eager.

'You didn't think you were done, did you?' he said, putting a hand on her hip and holding her still.

But what about him? She'd already…she'd already…

But that swirl of his tongue made any more thought impossible. And then his fingers pushed right into her slick heat. She arched taut, locking those talented fingers in place. But even then he teased. His mouth kept up that magic, sucking hard, while his tongue added rough slicks of pleasure. Unstoppable waves of heat rolled over her in a torrent of ecstasy. He growled against her in appreciative hunger as the convulsions started, applying more pressure with his fingers— pumping deeper, pressing harder against her inner walls, and he ate at her like she was the sweetest treat imaginable. Unbearable pleasure tore through her, harder this time as she squeezed on his hold and rode out the crest he'd conjured for her.

'*Leon!*'

It was a long moment before he answered, sliding up the bed, licking his lips and sending her a smug smile. 'Better now?'

He didn't expect an answer, did he? Because she was still struggling to return to reality, still catching her breath and still desperate for what more that was to come. She wanted *all* of him.

'This is you making the most of opportunities?' she eventually sighed, trying to keep it light even when she was almost buried in need for him.

His gaze turned smoky. 'Yes.'

'Please,' she muttered in total, helpless surrender.

That smokiness flared to fire—pure, burning lust. He thrust back off the bed and pretty much shredded his clothes. He reached into the drawer of the bedside cabinet and retrieved a condom.

'Don't worry,' he muttered. 'I have plenty.'

She trembled with anticipation—her mouth drying as she watched him. He was very…*well built*, and so highly aroused the sight of him made other parts of her moisten. He knelt on the bed and looked at her. He was a hot, experienced, sexually demanding man and right now he was motionless again—*thinking*.

The sexual suspense was almost killing her.

'How do you want…?' She trailed off. She had such little experience, she had no idea what to suggest.

'You have a list in mind?' he teased with a half-smile. ''Cos I do.'

'You go first, then,' she muttered in a low voice, blushing—and then blushing harder as she realised she blushed all over.

'Oh, *glykia mou*,' he chuckled. 'This first time I'm watching every moment flicker over your beautiful face.' He braced himself over her, running his hand down her side in a manner both soothing and stirring as he looked into her eyes. 'I want to see everything, feel everything...'

She felt a flash of vulnerability but he pressed closer and she could see him too—into those brown eyes that she knew had such depths. Right now, she saw desire and humour and the sharp bite of hunger.

'Then do what you want,' she whispered.

He kissed her into softness and stirring heat again. She couldn't believe this was happening. He overwhelmed her—his size, his heat, his musky scent.

'Breathe,' he muttered, gently probing her tightness. At the catch of her breath he hesitated and gave her a searching look.

'It's been a while,' she mumbled, burning with both desire and insecurity.

Another emotion flared in his eyes—hotter than ever. 'I know.'

He knew? How—because she was so desperate? Because she barely knew what she was doing?

'Relax. Kiss me.'

He lifted her, nudging her legs further apart so

she could take him more easily. Then in one smooth movement he kissed her and thrust deep at the same time. She cried out with the shocking pleasure of it and clutched his hips to keep him there.

'Okay?' he growled.

'Mmm-hmm.' She was almost delirious with the delight of it—he felt so heavy, she so full.

And it didn't just feel good, it also felt *right*. For the first time she actually understood why people liked this so much. He muttered something she didn't understand and crushed her closer.

And *this* was what she'd wanted most of all—him with her as completely as anyone could be. He moved, watching her, kissing her, riding her swiftly to that point beyond thought. It was unbearably awesome. She gave herself up to complete hedonism, not caring about anything but the demands of her body—driving her hips in the way instinct dictated she must. His breathing roughened, the glitter in his eyes sharpened.

'Ettie.' He huffed her name harshly and pumped harder.

She curled about him more tightly still, screaming as she came harder and longer than she could bear. She heard his roar of need and felt the sudden, full force of his lust unleashed. He slammed into her. Again, then again and again until they collided, interlocked, shaking together for a sublime moment of eternity, lost in that realm of total ecstasy.

She couldn't breathe. Couldn't believe.

'We're doing that again,' he muttered rawly. 'Now.'

* * *

The dog was gone. Rubbing his sleep-fuzzed head, Leon glanced at the empty basket with a frown. Ettie must have woken early and taken him for a walk. Leon wished she'd woken him—he'd have gone with her. Or better still, delayed her a little longer. His body was hard and ready—despite the aches from the full-on, all-night best sex of his life. His curiosity was fully aroused too. For the first time in a long time, he wanted to know more about a woman.

He paced the penthouse, running his hand through his hair again, aching for her return. One night wasn't going to be enough. He'd guessed they'd be good together, but he'd not imagined quite how hot. He grimaced wryly at the condom wrappers littering the bedroom floor. They'd barely bothered with sleep. After that first intense experience, he'd lifted her into the shower and taken his time to soap her up—easing away the last of her shyness and exposing the sly humour he'd seen fleeting snatches of. He'd held off letting her get off until she whispered something she wanted him to do and learned she knew a few curse words too. Hell, in that moment he'd have done anything she asked. She was generous and sweet and funny and he wanted nothing more than to kiss her everywhere until she came all over again.

Half an hour passed and still she didn't return. A prickle of foreboding slid down his spine. Why hadn't she come back? The full quota of staff would be on shift by now and she hadn't wanted to be seen by any of them.

He stilled, irritated. Was he actually worried about her? And the damn dog?

Disliking the uncertainty, he showered and dressed, but once downstairs he stopped some distance from the concierge desk. Ettie was in her uniform—filling out that crisp monogrammed T-shirt and parading the prim black trousers that on her embodied sexiness. She hadn't seen him; she was too busy pacifying a puce-faced resident.

'I'm so sorry that happened.' She sent the resident her most charming smile. 'Don't you worry, I'll straighten it out with George—he doesn't need to know most of it.' She picked up the box on the desk. 'How about we get Joel to come up and help you lift the dresser back into place?'

It was Saturday. Was she supposed to be working? Even if she was, why hadn't she bothered to wake him and say goodbye? Anger burned beneath his skin, but he turned to leave, fishing out his phone as it pinged with a message.

At the sound of an almighty clatter he glanced back. She'd dropped whatever it was in that box. Now she was flushed in the face and completely avoiding looking in his direction. Which meant she'd seen him. Her obvious discomfort eased the chill in his bones. So she felt awkward? Good. So she should.

She'd sneaked out early this morning and was now attempting to act as if *nothing* had happened. While he could respect her need to keep her private life private, he wasn't going to ignore her. And where was Toby? He almost missed the sleepy thing.

Ettie wasn't butter-fingered. Ever. Yet she'd just dropped an entire box of old cutlery, creating the loudest crash ever heard in the lobby. And Leon Kariakis was here to witness it. Of course he was.

Perspiration slicked over her skin. She couldn't look at him, but she could still see him from the corner of her eye and apparently he was busy scrolling through some vitally important message on his phone. At least he wasn't laughing at her openly.

She'd woken up stupidly early this morning and got hit right in the head with the reality hammer. He was fast asleep beside her—a vision of hot, sleepy sex-god—and she instantly realised how completely out of her depth she was. The one and only other time she'd woken next to a man, it had turned into one of the worst days of her life. Her ex had rejected her in the most humiliating, personal of ways the morning after. And then he'd done it all over again in public. The last thing she needed was to hear even any of that horror again from Leon.

She'd lain there frozen, becoming more and more terrified of the moment when he'd wake and see her in the cold light of day and realise his mistake. Sleeping with the sexually clueless concierge girl?

Her blood had iced at the prospect of the inevitably awkward—*or worse*—goodbye that would ensue. She couldn't bear to have any discussion or polite platitudes.

In the end she hadn't been able to stand the anxious torture. She'd slipped from the bed, wriggled into her dress and run—taking Toby with her before he barked his need to go outside. She'd been terrified of bumping into someone she knew in the lift. Of course, it stopped before the basement, ending her chance to escape to the staff locker room unseen. Jess had entered with her trolley. She'd stared at Toby and then at her.

'You should wear your hair loose more often.' Jess had smiled brightly after a horribly silent moment. 'It looks lovely. I didn't realise how long it had got.'

That was because Ettie couldn't afford to get it cut. And Jess had been lying—it didn't look lovely, it hadn't even been its usual wavy mess, but totally tangled, mussed-up bed-hair. That model had been seen exiting Leon's apartment only the other day in that supposed lift-ride of shame…and now she was doing the same? She pushed away the public humiliation. It wasn't worse than the horror she'd escaped years ago.

But she just couldn't face Leon. Her skin almost blistered with embarrassment at the thought of awkwardly extricating herself from his apartment. Because the last thing she could remember from the night before was his throaty laughter as he'd taken her apart again at some insane hour of the morning and now she couldn't work out if he'd been laughing *with* her or *at* her. She'd been his light relief for the night. And hardly his toughest challenge…in fact she'd been so *easy* she'd almost come in the taxi.

He wouldn't want a repeat. He'd probably been feigning sleep and just hoping she'd leave quietly, right?

But with every step she took, the tenderness between her thighs reminded her of his skilful passion, as did the sensitivity of her skin at her collar from the gentle grazes from his evening shadow...

One night only.

And she was not letting anyone know. Ever.

And she was not going to be able to look him in the eye again either. Ever.

Naturally, it was at that exact moment that he walked up to her desk.

'Where's Toby?' he asked briskly.

She fiddled with the box of cutlery the earlier resident had wanted her to return to the shop he'd purchased it from and just knew the man was *not* smiling.

'Harold's neighbour was away yesterday and only learned about what happened this morning. She's asked to take Toby. She cares for him very much.'

'That makes sense.' His reply was clipped.

'Actually, a number of the residents offered to take Toby when they heard what had happened,' she said meaningfully. 'I think a lot would like the "no pets" rule to be lifted.'

She glanced up then and saw winter had returned to his deep brown eyes. There was no hint of the intimacies they'd shared in his expression. There was nothing at all but cool control.

'Why are you on duty? It's Saturday. Haven't you been working all week?' He fired the questions like bullets.

So that was a no to pets, then. And a no to any kind of smile.

'One of the others called in sick and, as I was here

early to check on Toby…' She glanced at Joel, working near by, concerned he could hear them.

'Of course.' Leon nodded. 'Thank you.'

'It really is the best thing, I think,' she babbled anxiously because he had such a remote expression in his eyes and she felt him distancing himself even as he stood there. 'He'll be well cared for. She knows him and…' She licked her lips, dying of mortification, and tried to smile. 'I'll have his things cleared from your apartment shortly.'

He shot her an ice-cool look. 'You'll send one of the porters?'

'Of course.' Nervously she nodded. Because he didn't want her back up there?

Of course he didn't. Could the earth just open up and swallow her whole? *Now?* She'd made the right decision to run.

The second Leon left, Ettie leaned against the desk and breathed out, appallingly weak at the knees. That was it. There'd been no real goodbye. Nor was there any glow of amusement in his eyes—no sense of shared intimacy. If anything she had the odd feeling she'd somehow let him down. But that was impossible, wasn't it? He'd had what he wanted. So had she. And now there was no need to have to talk about it or anything mortifying like that. They could just pretend it had never happened.

It was over.

CHAPTER FOUR

'WHERE'S ETTIE?' THE beautifully clad woman demanded an answer from the youngest concierge. *Joel*—according to his monogrammed shirt.

Leon paused at a distance, unable to resist listening in for the answer.

'I'm sorry, Ms Welby, Ettie is away sick.' Joel offered an apologetic smile.

The woman laughed. 'Ettie is never sick. Just as Ettie never takes holidays. Ettie is simply always here. That's her job.'

'Well, she's not here now,' Joel said firmly.

No, she wasn't. She hadn't been at the desk for the last two days. Leon had noticed. He'd more than noticed; he'd *missed* her—missed seeing her smile and hearing her lovely chat with the residents.

He'd tried to avoid the concierge desk as much as possible initially. Unfortunately, he'd soon discovered that it was the heart of the operation. He'd pushed back—spending long hours at his office headquarters, taking more meetings. But he'd always glanced over when he'd walked in. And as the weeks passed, he'd walked through the lobby a little more often than was really required. But she still didn't look at him.

And now, even though it had been over three weeks, even though he knew all he needed to, he couldn't bring himself to move out of the penthouse and go home. Ettie still irritated him—rather, the way he kept *thinking* about her still irritated him— and that was a problem, given what he'd discovered about the way Cavendish House was run.

Awareness of her absence—*two days running*— sharpened his curiosity. And a chill of warning slithered down his spine because he saw the protectiveness in Joel's eyes as he referred to Ettie being ill. The young guy was concerned about his colleague. So what was wrong with her exactly, if Ettie was never ill?

'May I help instead?' Joel asked the resident awkwardly. 'Ettie's been schooling me in sorting drycleaning, you know.'

But the woman dropped her bundle of clothing on the desk and leaned towards Joel. 'Is Ettie actually okay?'

She'd gone from demanding customer to concerned busybody in a flash. That the woman genuinely was concerned for Ettie underlined everything Leon had learned: that everyone adored Ettie and relied on her completely.

'She should be back tomorrow.' Joel's smile wasn't reassuring enough. 'Let me take this for you in the meantime.'

The woman scooped up the dresses with a laugh.

'Thanks, but I don't trust *anyone* except Ettie. I'll wait for her to return.'

'If you're sure, madam.'

'You know I am.' She turned and caught sight of Leon watching her and her expression lit up with a huge smile. 'Oh, Mr Kariakis, it's lovely to finally meet you. My name's Autumn; I'm in apartment twenty-three.'

Leon nodded. 'Is everything okay for you, Autumn?'

'Well, apparently Ettie is away sick, which is hopeless, because she runs this place, Mr Kariakis; I hope you're aware of that.'

He nodded. He'd rapidly become aware of the fact, as it happened. In every conversation he had with either resident or management, it was Ettie to whom they referred for fixing problems. Which was why the fact that he'd taken her to bed was more of a problem than he'd expected it would be. That and the fact that he still couldn't get her out of his head. 'I'm glad you appreciate the service the Cavendish offers.'

'I appreciate *Ettie*,' she said firmly. 'Ettie is simply the best.'

Yes, she was. He never should have slept with her.

'How long has she been away?' Leon asked Joel as idly as he could after Autumn had headed towards the lift.

'I'm sure she'll be back tomorrow,' Joel said with a valiant defence. 'Ettie's never sick.'

That didn't answer his question, but Leon let it slide. He'd give her until tomorrow to return; if she didn't, then he was going to have to investigate.

He couldn't stop thinking about her. It had only been one night and he'd had many one nights with many women, so why was he stuck thinking about *her*?

Was it simply because she now seemed to be missing? Why wasn't she at work? He disliked unanswered questions. Just as he disliked messy endings and tearful women. They were why he stuck to one night.

Ettie was the first woman who'd left *him*. No tears, no mess, no reference to it at all, in fact. If it hadn't been for the sweet scent of her lingering in the air, he might have imagined the whole thing. Except he dreamed of it every night too.

Not turning up to work wasn't something she often did. Nor were one-night stands. When he'd approached her in front of her colleagues that next day she'd been dying of mortification; he'd just been too annoyed to pay attention to it properly at the time. She was shy. Inexperienced. Sweet. And he was a fool for having lost his head and seducing her. Especially now it had become clear she was the main asset of this entire enterprise and he needed her to take more of a leading role.

A horrible thought hit him: was *he* the reason she was away now? Was she so embarrassed by what had happened she was off hunting for another job? Or had he hurt her in some way and not realised—was that why she'd run off so early that next morning? And how was it possible he felt the loss of that damn dog when he'd had custody over it for less than twenty-four hours?

A sharp memory impinged on his mind. A memory he'd blocked for years—of a tiny puppy he'd adored more than anything else in his life. Only it had been snatched away from him just as everything important had then. He'd been betrayed again by the most important person in his life. He swiftly, curtly reminded himself that pets, like people, were not permanent. The loss of them hurt. Which was why he kept them at a distance.

Emotions—all emotions—were a weakness. He'd learned that lesson long ago and he'd remember it well now. Never admit to them, never show them.

It was barely eight in the morning when he went down to the concierge desk the next day. He'd hardly slept. He wasn't going to rest properly until he knew. That fact irritated him. He didn't allow other people's problems to affect him. He didn't let his *own* problems affect him. He just fixed them.

'Still no Ettie?' he asked Joel bluntly.

'No, sir,' the concierge answered awkwardly. 'But she's never had a day off before in the entire time I've been here.'

Leon spied the battered book open on the desk and recognised Ettie's handwriting. He reached across and spun it round to flick through the pages.

'They're Ettie's lists,' Joel hurriedly explained. 'She designed the systems for us. This is our bible.'

Leon knew exactly what it was. She was insanely over-competent. But basic details were all he needed. A phone number, an address. And, as he'd suspected, Ettie had the staff roster in the back of her book. And, with the roster, full contact details. Feeling like some gumshoe detective—*or stalker*—he employed his photographic memory and left.

The drive took longer than he'd guessed it would. She had to spend a while on the trains in the mornings and evenings, which meant that on those nights she worked her other job she got home horribly late. He climbed the stairs of the rundown housing block, trying not to judge the grime and smell. He knew he was from a privileged background. He was luckier than almost every other damn person in the world. Quelling his concerns for her personal security, he knocked on the door. A few moments later, he heard the locks being pulled back.

'Mr Kariakis?'

Leon tensed. He hadn't been Mr Kariakis when she'd been screaming her pleasure beneath him. But he shoved the resentment aside, because she looked horribly unwell.

'What are you doing here?' She peered past him as if expecting to see someone else. 'Has something happened?'

'What's wrong?' He pushed the words out.

It was a searing pleasure to see her, but he was also hit with a sharp pain at how fragile she looked… Her eyes were huge in her pale face and she was swamped in an ancient woollen jumper, black leggings beneath, warm wool socks on her feet.

'Do you need me back at work?' She looked so guilty and anxious, he felt bad.

'Of course not,' he said curtly, keen to dismiss her guilt. 'Not when you're clearly ill.'

Her eyes widened. 'Did you think I wasn't?'

He drew in a sharp breath. 'Ettie,' he growled. 'Invite me in.'

She didn't want to—that truth was written all over her beautifully expressive face. But she stepped to the side. The atmosphere intensified as she closed the door behind him. Something was bundled up inside him too tightly and he had to turn away from her.

She lived in a small, dingy apartment. There was no television, just books, and an old laptop on the dining table. He noticed an instrument case on the bookshelf together with a pile of sheet music. The sofa looked old and lumpy. But she'd tried to brighten the place up with a throw and cushions and three little pot plants on the narrow windowsill. It was immaculately clean and tidy. That made sense.

He'd seen the organisation and management systems she'd put in place for the concierge desk. Everything was written up neatly—processes and information. Perfection. No wonder every resident had been asking where she was these past few days.

'You noticed my absence?' she asked huskily.

He'd noticed her absence when he'd woken that morning and found her gone. He'd been noticing it ever since. 'I was concerned you might have been embarrassed about what happened between us. I didn't want that affecting your ability or desire to remain at Cavendish House.'

Her chin lifted. 'I'm not ashamed. And I'm not pining after you, if that's what you were thinking.'

'No.' He almost smiled because hadn't that been one little wish? 'So you're not planning on leaving Cavendish?'

Her brow furrowed. 'Did you think I was off having interviews or something?' She shook her head. 'Of course not. I love my residents.'

He stilled. He should have remembered that about her—loyalty, *passion*. That tension soared. It took everything he had not to take two steps and haul her into his arms.

'How did you find out where I live?' she asked, wrapping her arms around herself in a self-conscious gesture.

'I might've looked at your personnel roster.' He glanced at her.

She still looked shell-shocked and paler than he could've imagined. He had the urge to scoop her off her feet and abduct her. He'd take her back to his apartment, he'd...*what*?

Leon gritted his teeth. Not appropriate. Not allowed.

Ettie swallowed hard, still unable to believe Leon Kariakis was standing in the middle of her tiny flat. It was mortifying. Worse than that, it was...*exciting* in an appalling, illicit way. She'd wondered if she was hallucinating when she'd first answered the door. Now adrenaline surged and she fought not to be driven towards his innate sensuality, fought to settle the sizzle stirring in her blood. Yet her heart beat with more vigour than it had in weeks.

It's not why he's here.

'It was nice of you to be concerned, but it's just a stomach bug,' she said unevenly. 'I think the worst is over now, but you don't want to catch it.'

Please leave. Please leave.

Before she did something stupid like throw herself at him.

'You're sure you shouldn't see a doctor?' He frowned at her.

'No, truly. I just need a little more sleep.'

That customary stillness settled over him as he stared at her. 'Ettie.' His voice was little more than a whisper.

She froze, mentally replaying that soft call to her. Had she heard what she so desperately wanted to hear in his voice? Had there been something more than concern? Had there been longing?

Because of the size of her flat, he was delightfully— dangerously—close. She dragged in a sharp breath, straining to resist. It would be so easy to reach up and kiss him.

You can't.

If she did, she'd be lost. She wasn't cut out to cope with an affair with a man like him. What he'd made her feel that night? She'd be an addict in no time— desperate to have her fix even at the expense of her own well-being. She couldn't afford to be a stupid romantic like her mother—always falling for the wrong guy. The guy who'd never love her back. Leon Kariakis didn't do relationships, he did challenges. Regret swamped her.

If only...

She'd written down the pros and cons and lit a match to send the paper up in smoke. Even so, that lopsided list was burned on her brain. She knew the reality and her responsibility.

'I *need* my job...' She was reminding herself more than telling him. 'I'm sorry to have troubled you. You didn't need to come all the way out here.' Her words were at odds with her secret want. She wanted him to have come here because *he'd* needed—*her*.

'No trouble,' he said stiffly, distance evident in his stance again. 'And you don't need to worry. I'm not about to ask for anything...*inappropriate*.'

He wasn't? Great. Now she was even more mortified by her slight assumption that there'd been any *personal* element to this visit. He valued her more as a concierge than as a concubine. He had no 'best lover ever' award for her—though he'd certainly won hers.

Now he strode to the door, his long pace leashed. He almost looked angry. 'I'll be implementing some changes at Cavendish House. We can discuss them when you get back.'

She nodded, unable to speak because a stupidly large lump had sprung up in her throat.

'But you're not to return until you're fully fit,' he added as an afterthought. 'Everything can wait until then.'

But it couldn't wait.

Because she'd missed her shift at the stationery shop, her boss had released her from all duties there—dismissing her with immediate effect. As she

wasn't on contract, just a relief worker, she had little recourse but to suck it up. The tummy bug had
eased—she'd stopped vomiting, though she still felt
horrible and horrendously tired. That was too bad.
She had to get back to work. Three days off had been
an indulgence too far.

She needed the money. And she needed the distraction.

'What's been happening?' she quickly asked Joel as
she stepped behind the Cavendish House concierge
desk first thing the next morning.

Joel didn't have the chance to reply because Leon
Kariakis was bearing down on them both, his expression shockingly thunderous. Oddly his jaw was
shadowed, as if he'd not shaved for a day.

'What are you doing here?' His cold, furious gaze
sliced right through her.

'What does it look like I'm doing?' Ettie summoned the biggest fake smile she could muster. She
was keeping things professional. Maintaining distance. Doing her job.

'You're not working today,' Leon snapped. 'Turn
around and go home. I'll hail a taxi.'

Ettie gaped, then glared at him. Had he *no* thought
for privacy? And as if she could ever afford to go all
the way home in a cab!

'Excuse me a moment, please, Joel.' She stalked
into the small office, not bothering to see if Leon followed her. Because of course he did.

'What are *you* doing?' she threw at him the second he'd closed the door.

'Ettie.' It was a soft growl.

It was the almost irritated look of concern in his eyes that devastated her. She had to turn away from it. But he grabbed her shoulders and turned her back, tilting her chin up. Not so he could steal a kiss, but to subject her to his disapproving inspection. His frown deepened. 'You've lost weight. You shouldn't be here at all today. Not for the rest of the week.'

'I'm fine,' she argued, burning at his touch, at the tension tearing her apart every time she so much as thought about him. Which was insanely often. And to see him? To be this close to him? She was going to have to find a new job after all.

'You're pale. Have you had breakfast?' He interrogated her grimly.

'I need to be here. I need to work.'

'You still look awful.'

'And thank you for that,' she muttered. 'I'm *fine*. It's my decision, Leon. Not your concern.'

An indefinable emotion whipped across his face and then he froze. 'Not my concern?' he echoed with lethal softness.

'You value your independence as much as I do and don't try to argue otherwise,' she said. 'If you needed to work, you would. And I need to work.'

'Not today—'

'I have no sick leave left,' she snapped. 'The stationery shop has given me the boot because I missed shifts this week, and I need the money because

Ophelia has unforeseen expenses. I *am* working today and you are *not* stopping me. Nor are you offering to help me,' she burst out, rejecting his offer before he could make it. Because she just knew he would make it now she'd told him all that. 'I don't want any help from you.'

His mouth opened and shut again as he visibly sought for control. But then he lost it. 'Damn your pride, Ettie,' he ground out in a low voice.

He ran a frustrated hand through his hair, his customary coolness evaporating in a swirl of motion. 'There's independent. And then there's stubborn and pig-headed. You're the latter.'

The guy had no concept of talking quietly. He was all orders and commands and shouting. Joel could probably hear him on the other side of the door, and it would be around the staff that she and Leon Kariakis and were alone in the office, arguing like…like… *lovers.*

'Shush,' she whispered furiously.

'Did you just shush me?' His gaze glittered.

'I have to get on with my job. Please, Leon,' she suddenly broke and begged, her voice catching. 'Leave me alone.'

Leon was silenced. And furious. She couldn't be any clearer. She didn't want him around. But he knew she did. He could see the desperation in her eyes now—she was positively drinking him in.

'What are you doing?' Her voice wavered as he stalked nearer.

Behaving badly. Doing what they both wanted.

What they both needed. He hadn't slept a wink since
seeing her yesterday, his temper was ragged and he'd
been under extreme restraint for too long. Her chin
was stuck in the air and her 'leave me alone' vibes
couldn't hum louder. He wasn't going to linger where
he wasn't wanted.

Except he knew he *was* wanted. Very much. He
could see it in her luminous, emotion-laden green
eyes, and those vibes had a strong bass thrum of desire. But she had irritatingly strong willpower. She
didn't want to want him any more. Well, that made
two of them. Because he'd never wanted to be held
hostage to desire like this. Never wanted to feel this
need to know she was okay. To be so shockingly concerned about her appearance.

She was so beautiful. But right now she looked unbearably fragile. Pale and interesting didn't suit Ettie—
she was meant to be full of vitality and radiance.

'Leon.' Her whisper wasn't one of rejection. It was
a plea.

He was desperate to get her out of his head, the
want for her out of his blood. Never before had he
wasted time thinking about anything other than work.
He'd never let himself want something so much it
became a complete distraction. He controlled all his
emotions—even desire.

So now he didn't kiss her. He couldn't. Not when
she'd asked him not to. But he'd allow himself just
the smallest, gentlest of touches. As he spanned her
waist, he heard not just a hitch in her breathing, but
also a stifled moan. He felt the ripple of yearning

arch through her body and he pulled her closer into his embrace. A hug, right?

But desire burgeoned between them. He gazed into her eyes, watching the searing craving build. Neither could hide it. Nor deny it.

'You don't want any help from me?' he growled at her. 'But you still want me.'

Her soft mouth parted, her lips full and reddened. But her eyes pleaded with him—tormenting him with two vastly different requests. 'That's different.'

It was. And it complicated everything.

She didn't want to want him. Well, *ditto*. With every ounce of willpower he could summon, he released her and stalked out of the room.

Ettie's heart plummeted as the door slammed behind him. She'd *craved* more contact with him. That need had been constant since that first night. No matter how hard she'd fought against it the want simply grew. And now?

She'd banished him for good.

She breathed in and out, trying to steady her pulse and ignore the sharp pain high in her chest. Eventually the adrenaline burst vanished, leaving her overwhelmingly exhausted.

It was so stupid to still feel so tired. She'd not lied to Leon, she'd slept like a log last night, but she just couldn't seem to get enough rest despite turning in as early as she could. She had no idea how she was going to rearrange Autumn Welby's massive walk-in wardrobe right now. Autumn liked her to do it every month and usually it was fine—enjoyable even—to see the dazzling dresses. But this morning the thought of sorting out all those evening gowns made her arms ache and the prospect of Autumn's perfume collection made her gag even more.

'You okay, Ettie?' Joel frowned as she walked from the concierge office to the lift. 'Need a coffee?' He held out a mug.

'No, thanks. I'm fine,' she lied.

In truth she was hot, cold and queasy and the strong smell of coffee almost made her retch. The lift dinged and the doors slid open but Ettie didn't step in. She'd never felt so awful in her life.

'Ettie?' Joel called to her again.

She turned her head to answer him, but then she heard someone else.

'Ettie? *Ettie!*' Leon was shouting.

Blindly she reeled as her body pulsed with regret and *longing*. She opened her mouth to reply but it was too late; nothing came out.

CHAPTER FIVE

'ETTIE…'

It was the merest whisper, but it was that same
voice she'd heard in the moment before everything
went black.

Leon.

Blinking rapidly, she tried to sit up, but he firmly
pushed her back down onto the plush sofa. She shivered at the contact, goose bumps lifting all over her
skin. It was appalling how much she wanted that
touch.

'Stay still,' he ordered tightly.

He was leaning so close, he was all she could see.
Bossy as ever. He'd taken off his jacket, and in his
crisp white shirt and dark tie he looked stunning. But
it was his eyes that made her all but limp—the po-
tency and depth of the brown and the heat in the amber
lights. How had she ever thought his gaze was cool?

It wasn't a ripple of forbidden desire that slithered
down her spine now, it was a tsunami. Her body was
a disgrace to her—a confused mess. Unwell one moment, racked with feverish lust the next.

'Leon…' She murmured the all too obvious like some brainless devotee. She'd ached to see him again. Then she remembered. She'd fainted at his feet. What an *idiot*.

He looked more serious than ever, which ought to have been impossible. 'I told you, you're still unwell.'

'I've just…' She trailed off.

'It's gone on too long, Ettie,' Leon said decisively.

She struggled against the sneaking desire to lean against him. Instead she made herself look past him. Where was she? Not the concierge office because there was no sofa in there.

'I'm in your penthouse.' Her pulse spiked as she realised.

'Yes.'

'Why?'

'Because you fainted in the lobby.'

'No, I meant… I could have gone into the office.' She moistened her dry lips with her tongue. He hadn't needed to bring her up here. *How* had she got up here? Her heart sank and soared at the same time. He'd carried her. She just knew it.

'Too bad for you.' His tone was cool.

It was too bad, because she still wanted him even when it was impossible. And so damn embarrassing. She shut her eyes to block out the intensity of his impact on her, but somehow it just made it worse. She could *feel* his heat and strength. 'I don't mean to be ungrateful.'

'Leave it, Ettie,' he said softly. 'The doctor's on her way.'

Her eyes flashed open. 'A doctor? I don't need a doctor. I just need another day in bed…'

He was so very near and at her words something stirred in his eyes. Physical weakness sapped her will-power. *His* bed was very near. His bed, where he'd made her feel *everything*.

Her mouth dried as her skin sizzled. Her yearning multiplied to the point of madness. And he knew her thoughts, didn't he? Because he leaned closer, his hand sliding through her hair as he cupped her head and searched her eyes.

'I'm probably infectious,' she mumbled, a final, hopeless defence.

She'd become a little challenge for him again, that was all.

'Too late. I think I've already got it,' he replied grimly. 'Feverish. Sleepless. Loss of appetite…'

Her heart pounded so hard it was a wonder it didn't snap her ribs. 'Leon—'

A loud knock on the door dragged his attention from her and his too rare smile flashed even as he groaned. 'Just in time…'

Ettie pulled herself into a sitting position while Leon answered the door. She heard a concise conversation in Greek and didn't understand a word.

'Ettie, this is Dr Notaras,' Leon said briskly, returning to the lounge followed by a tall, glamorous brunette. 'I'll just be in the study. Call me when you're done.' He said that last to the doctor.

Ettie smiled wanly at the terrifyingly skilled woman and tried to tell her she was fine, but the doctor wasn't all that interested in what Ettie had to say initially. She was too busy taking her temperature and looking in her ears and mouth.

'You've not got any fever,' the doctor noted with a cautious expression. 'And there's no sign of any ear or throat infection. Nothing in the chest. Your pulse is strong, blood pressure good.' She then asked a few questions about her background—no diabetes or history of heart problems?

Ettie shook her head. But what about the nausea? And her sensitivity to some smells?

'Is there any chance you could be pregnant?' the doctor asked blandly.

'N…' She broke off.

There was only one, impossible chance. Although…

She pressed her lips together to stop herself stuttering. There'd been more than one *chance* in that one magical night. Her brain kickstarted into frantic overdrive—desperately searching her memory for dates, signs, *denial*. Finally she seized on the only important fact she could bear to consider. They'd used protection. Every time, right?

'I have a home test in my bag and I can take bloods right now…' the doctor said with quiet efficiency after Ettie's lengthy silence had spoken volumes.

'I can investigate that possibility on my own,' Ettie whispered with a shake of her head. She needed to get away from Leon and find out for herself.

But the doctor searched in her bag for a second and then handed Ettie a slim foil package. She gave Ettie her contact card as well.

'Get in touch if you'd like to see me again. It's truly no problem.' The doctor gave her a professional, but sincere smile.

Ettie had the horrendous feeling it was a huge problem.

'I can come to wherever you are,' the doctor said encouragingly. 'Any time. Leon said—'

'This is just between us, right?' Ettie interrupted swiftly. This woman wasn't about to tell Leon pregnancy was even a possibility, was she?

'Of course.' The doctor nodded and stood.

'Thank you.'

Dr Notaras called something in Greek and Ettie quickly put the slim package into her pocket. She wasn't discussing this with Leon; there was no need. Because it *was* impossible, wasn't it?

She heard more rapid Greek and the lift chime. A few moments later Leon walked back into the lounge alone. He didn't look any less serious, or any more relieved.

'I should get back downstairs.' She couldn't look him in the eye.

'You're staying here,' he replied curtly.

'Leon—'

'If you go back down, I'll cart you straight back up here again even if you scream at me to stop. I don't care who stares.'

Furious at his high-handedness, she determinedly stood in a swift movement. 'I have a job to do and I'm perfectly capable of doing it.'

'What's this?'

Ettie glanced down. The pregnancy test had fallen from her pocket and with his damn panther-like reflexes he'd picked it up before she'd even registered it had tumbled.

'It was just something the doctor…' She trailed off, clenching her fists tightly as he read the print on the packet.

He looked from the test to her. His face had actually whitened beneath his olive-toned skin and his eyes narrowed. 'Is this a possibility?'

She couldn't reply; she was too shocked to see him looking so *appalled*. Her pulse skittered. He didn't want this. He really, *really* didn't want this. Well, nor did she. She breathed in and out, but couldn't think for the noise of her blood pounding in her ears.

'Ettie?' he snapped.

She shook her head. 'We used protection.'

Leon's breath hissed out between his gritted teeth. Her plea granted the smallest peace in his sea of panic. It revealed she'd only him to consider, only that one night. There was no other man in her life and she'd not slept with anyone else in a long time. But then he'd known that the night he'd been with her. She'd been shy and sweet and definitely not especially experienced. The expression of rapture and amazement on her face when she'd come in his arms haunted him. He wanted to make her respond like that again; he'd been aching to do that for weeks.

But now?

The fear in her eyes only grew. 'I just can't be pregnant. Not to—'

'Me?' He frowned. Yeah, even she instinctively knew he wasn't father material. His blood chilled. 'Sorry, Ettie. I know there aren't any other possibilities for the baby's paternity.'

She swallowed but didn't deny it.

'Go and do the pregnancy test,' he ordered. He needed to know. Now.

Her hand shook as she took the package from him. He could all but see her brain processing, frantically remembering dates, the dawning realisation that it might be real. That maybe the reason she'd been feeling rotten wasn't from any infection.

Why hadn't she told him just now? What would have happened had he still been away? If he hadn't been here to see her faint? Would she have told him once she knew? Horror burned. This was everything he didn't want. Flickering memories stirred—of the childhood he'd hated. Of loneliness and lack of power. Everything he didn't want.

He paced the room as he waited. He had to get on top of this situation. *Now.*

She couldn't look at him when she returned from the bathroom. She didn't speak either. She just sat back down on the sofa and drew her feet up until she was in a small ball. An intense pressure built in his chest. But he leaned against the wall and waited, even though he already knew.

'It can't be right,' she said in a whisper. 'We used protection.'

He stared at her fixedly. 'Nothing is one hundred per cent fail-proof.'

'Abstinence is,' she muttered grimly.

Her answer offered a wisp of amusement. 'You know that wasn't an option that night.'

She lifted her lashes, her eyes revealing her distress. 'We're talking lifelong consequences, Leon.'

So she was going to have the baby. One swirling chunk of unease settled within him.

'What are you thinking?' he asked as calmly as he was able. Which was frankly nothing on his usual impassive façade.

She shied away from looking at him again.

'Ettie?' His almost customary cool rose a few degrees. This was so personal, so deeply troubling, he couldn't keep his equanimity. Because it wasn't quite up to him any more.

'I need some space.' She tried to stand up but her face turned grey.

'Sit down.' He was furious with her.

'It'll pass,' she snapped.

And just like that the atmosphere flared, leaping right into dangerous. *Emotional.*

'Most probably. But until it does, you stay right where you are.' He huffed out a tight breath. 'You're not going back to work today.' He threw out a gesture to close down the immediate argument in her eyes. 'Give this today at least, damn it.'

They both breathed out harshly. And then she sank back down to sit on the sofa again.

'It was a night for me,' she muttered fiercely. 'Just for *me*. Just one night. And now this.'

'I'm sorry.' And he truly was. He knew she didn't

do one-night stands. He knew she wasn't all that experienced. And the one time she'd let herself go? 'You've got to tell me what you're thinking.'

Because she was thinking—overthinking—if the tight expression on her face was anything to go by. A myriad of emotions flickered in her eyes, but mostly misery.

Finally she turned towards him, squaring her slim shoulders. 'I'm going to have the baby.'

Yes, he'd known that she would.

But then she spoke some more. 'You don't have to…'

A fierce fury enveloped him as she started to negate his input. 'I don't have to *what*?'

Her lack of answer sent him on the attack. 'You doubt I'd want to be involved?'

'You can't even bring yourself to take a dog for a walk,' she flared up. 'How are you going to meet a baby's needs?'

'I only said I couldn't walk the dog because I wanted to see more of you,' he ground out. 'You know it was my excuse to get you up to my penthouse.'

Her eyes widened and her mouth opened. But she remained speechless. He glared right back at her. She really *hadn't* known that?

He muttered something unprintable beneath his breath. 'I wanted you the second I laid eyes on you, Ettie. And it was the same for you. Frankly, I still want you. Isn't that a good place for us to begin this?'

Her mouth hung open for another moment. Then

she snapped it shut and vehemently shook her head. 'There is no *this*. And *that* doesn't last.'

Didn't it? Because it had already lasted longer for her than for any other woman in his life.

He stilled, rapidly reassessing his strategy. He had a highly developed capacity to think through all possible problems, combinations, options in a situation… and he was equally swift to sift and find solutions. An unplanned pregnancy was the antithesis of his life's ambition. He'd never wanted a child. Never wanted a long-term relationship. He'd never even considered it. But fate in the form of a failed condom was forcing both upon him.

He could barely bring himself to think of an actual baby. It was too tiny, too vulnerable. He wouldn't even know how to hold the thing. He ran a hand through his hair and dragged back his focus. He'd do what he was good at—*management*.

While he could provide many important things—wealth, home, an elite education…those things weren't what really mattered. But he'd ensure it had everything he hadn't had. Safety. Security…

He glanced back up and saw her sitting on that sofa—her arm already curved across her flat belly in an instinctive, unconsciously protective maternal gesture as she watched him with a very wary expression on her face.

For only a second did he brood on those old, darkest of memories. The fear, the pain, the isolation. His mother had hated him and she'd shown it in almost every action of almost every day.

But Ettie would be a good mother. Probably too good, given that she put everyone else ahead of herself. She did everything within her power for those she loved.

But it was a shame that it had happened so soon for her and with him of all people. Guilt sucked the strength from his bones. He never should have seduced her. He'd been selfish and greedy and now changed her life irrevocably. Because that baby she was carrying was his.

His inner animal wanted to beat his chest and roar. He'd not stopped wanting her in these past few weeks but he'd been determined to do the right thing. He'd kept his distance, respected her wishes…not messed more personally with his latest business acquisition. He'd tried to restore his own control and not break those rules all over again. But this changed everything.

It was very simple now. The baby would have Ettie. And Ettie would have him.

And there was only one tolerable course of action to ensure that: *marriage*.

It would be an amicable, workable arrangement— basically an acquisition like any other. They just needed to hammer out the terms, come to an agreement and settle it.

But, given the way she was freaking out in front of him, she was going to resist. He was going to have to go gently with her. One thing he'd learned in his business dealings was that in a takeover the acquisition generally loathed being ordered to do something.

'I want to go home.' She glanced at him and defiance shone in her eyes. 'I need some space.'

Leon bit his tongue. Hard. She wasn't staying in that hellhole of an apartment a moment longer.

'This is a shock,' he said after a moment. 'But we're going to figure a way through it. I am trying really hard here not to...'

'Take total control?' she guessed coldly. 'Keep trying.'

He glared at her and made himself draw in another steadying breath. 'I'd like you to live with me,' he said. 'I'd like not to have to worry about you when you're not here.'

'You'd worry that I wasn't doing a good enough job alone?' She got defensive.

He bit back a growl and tried to take even more care over his words. 'You're very good at taking care of other people. Yourself, not so much.'

'I've looked after Ophelia all my life. And myself. I can take care of it,' she said defiantly. 'It's my baby.'

Her statement of claim sent sparks through his blood. There was the fierce tigress—all passion and protectiveness—but he was every bit as protective.

'Mine too,' he shot back. Screw gentle. 'And *we* will take care of it.'

The look she sent him was pure mistrust and it was so damn unwarranted, it riled him more. 'We're equally responsible, so we'll handle this together.'

She looked away.

He got it. He did. Or he tried to. She was used to taking care of everything by herself. He didn't know much about her mother, but he got that Ettie, the child, had been the responsible one. She'd been the primary carer for her whole little family. But she needed to understand that he wasn't going anywhere.

'I will not abandon you,' he ground edgily through gritted teeth. 'And you're not staying in that damp apartment. That's not happening.'

'It's my home.'

Not any more. 'You'll move in with me. Immediately.'

'You're not even asking now,' she said in an accusatory tone. 'You're dictating.'

'Yeah.'

She stared at him, clearly shocked by his unashamed affirmation of the fact.

'I'm not tiptoeing around, Ettie. Be where you need to be.' He shrugged. 'I'm not going anywhere and nor are you.'

Her fragility frightened him, her resistance frustrated him. His own wants made him grouchiest of all. He wanted her in his bed but he couldn't have that now. He'd have this sorted instead. It was an easy enough fix if they could both keep their cool. He'd tried to reassure her and take it slow, but he was used to giving orders and having them instantly obeyed. 'You're not going to wake up in the morning and find me gone.'

Her skin flooded with colour. Because yeah, that was exactly what she'd done to him. He strode over and hunched down in front of her, striking while he had the advantage. 'We'll get engaged.'

'We'll *what*?' She actually shrank back from him.

'I don't want everyone thinking you're just my live-in lover or latest affair; I want you to have more status than that.' He drew in another deep breath but it did little to take the edge off the irritation that was festering with her refusal.

'Oh,' she said poisonously. 'Because as your fiancée I'd have *so* much *status*.' Her words simply dripped with sarcasm.

'Ettie,' he couldn't help a half-laugh, 'don't be a witch.' He leaned closer. 'I want this child to be legitimate. It should have its rightful inheritance. This is *my* reputation as well as yours.'

She wrinkled her nose. 'You care about your reputation?'

'I keep my personal life discreet.' His personal life generally consisted of pleasurable screws with swift conclusions. 'I'm seen as reliable for my investors. That matters to my business.'

And he was certain it mattered to her. She was afraid he'd abandon her—well, this was one way of showing he wasn't about to. 'We'll get a ring and announce our engagement—'

'I'm *not* getting engaged again,' she blurted, before blushing beetroot.

'Again?' Leon stilled as her words sank in and a balloon of outrage burst in his gut. 'You've been engaged before?'

CHAPTER SIX

ETTIE SEEMED TO have frozen in place on the sofa. 'We don't know each other at all, Leon. This just can't work.'

'Tell me what happened,' Leon said grimly.

'It doesn't matter what happened,' she snapped.

'Obviously it does, because it's rendering you irrational now.'

'Me irrational? You're the crazy one—insisting on marriage when it's completely unnecessary.'

Actually, it was imperative. The more he thought about it, the more crucial the concept had become.

But she leapt up from the sofa and paced away from him. 'I'm not going through that humiliation again,' she muttered. 'I'm no longer that stupid, naive girl who believed in happy-ever-after.'

Her vehemence drew a smile from him. 'You believed in happy-ever-after?'

She lifted her chin in the face of his amusement. 'Why shouldn't I have?' But then she blushed again and turned away as some bitter memory made her face fall. 'Forget it.'

He considered her words quickly—*humiliation, naivety.* 'He broke up with you?'

She nodded.

He didn't press for more details. Now wasn't the time. 'I'm not promising you moon dust,' he said with simple clarity. 'I'm not declaring undying devotion. We'll have no lies. No false promises.' He drew in a breath as the perfect plan crystallised in his mind. 'Don't think of this as a traditional marriage proposal. This isn't romantic love, rainbows and unicorns, this is a real solution to a real issue,' he said. 'Obviously I'll financially support both you and the baby one hundred per cent. That's a given. But here's my offer. If you marry me, I will pay for all of Ophelia's schooling. Not just the rest of this year, but all her university studies as well. She wants to do medicine, correct? So a decade or thereabouts of training and specialisation? Paid for. She doesn't have to stress about getting a scholarship, she just needs to be accepted onto the course. She can choose any university—hell, any country; if she wants to do some parts of it in the States, Europe…that's fine. All fees, all accommodation costs, living costs, everything. I have it covered. She only has to get the grades.'

He paused, watching intently for her response.

She was motionless, her clear-eyed gaze fixed upon him. 'You can't possibly—'

'Say the word and I'll have my lawyer draw up the contract. I do not enter contracts lightly, Ettie. And I do not break them. This is a legitimate offer. All you have to do is accept it.'

'By marrying you.' Her focus wavered.

'Yes.'

'But we don't love each other.'

'That's irrelevant.' He dismissed the concern with ruthless efficiency. This wasn't about anything emotional, this was about security, practicality, plain common sense.

She swallowed. 'You would expect us to remain married...for good?'

Something stirred low in his gut at her question. He ignored it. 'I don't see why it shouldn't work out long-term. However, if things became difficult between us personally, then we'd find an alternative solution. My financial commitment to your sister wouldn't be broken, however. Nor to you. As the mother of my child, you will always have a home.'

Ettie reeled. He made it sound like she'd won the lottery. 'Why can't we find that alternative solution now?'

'Because I will not allow my child to be born illegitimately,' he reiterated sharply. 'However, I don't imagine that things would become difficult. We work together well, Ettie.'

Work together? He really saw this as an emotionless, uncomplicated resolution? Obviously for him it was exactly that. Because apparently it wouldn't be the 'done thing' for him to have an illegitimate child with a service worker...

And he was playing on her loyalty and love for her sister to get what he wanted. It was ruthless of him. But she suddenly realised that that was what he did—targeted an acquisition and did what it took to make the deal happen. And he did it damn fast. No wonder he'd made all that money by such a young age.

'You know I can support you, Ettie. I have the finances and the wherewithal to ensure both you and the baby have everything you need,' he said firmly.

The shutters on Ettie's bruised heart closed. 'The baby will need more than financial security.'

She needed more too. Because she knew happiness came from something other than money. But she had the feeling she wasn't about to get it.

'Of course, but the basics in life also matter. Food, clothing, decent accommodation.'

His cold emphasis on the latter irked her enough to spell it out. 'What about emotional security?'

'You already love the baby.'

His simple, swift assertion silenced her and to her horror tears sprang to her eyes. Because in that instant she realised she did. As shockingly unexpected, as inconvenient, as *new* as it all was…it was wonderful. Raw emotion swept over her at the thought of that tiny little being growing inside her. Their baby. Her imagination sprang into overtime, sending her images of a beautiful child—a female Leon, or maybe a mini-me little boy… If this baby had half Leon's looks, it was going to melt every heart.

'Write the list, Ettie.' He was watching her coolly as if analysing her every word, every expression. 'All the reasons for, all the reasons against. Make your decision from there.'

There was no 'decision' and he knew it. The arrangement he'd offered was impossible for her to refuse. Because it wasn't about her. It was about this tiny baby. And it was about Ophelia. Leon was offering complete security for them both. Ophelia could just relax and focus on her studies without the added pressure of trying to get a scholarship. He'd said she could apply to any university and Ettie knew he meant it. It was incredibly generous…

But Leon didn't really want *her*. It had been a one-night-stand—that was all he'd wanted. And she'd lived with the consequences of a one-night stand. Her sister, Ophelia.

She and Ophelia had both been unwanted by their fathers. She'd watched her mother become embittered by the betrayal of the men she'd wanted to love…to the point where she no longer coped with the normal demands of life. And Ettie had been a fool for love too, hadn't she? Flattered by the first man to pay her attention… She'd been such an idiot. And now?

Leon Kariakis didn't actually want anything from her. He had more money than he knew what to do with and he had an endless stream of willing women. He was simply stuck with her and being honourable about it—saying all the right things, attempting to do the right things. But wasn't that only going to lead to resentment in the end? He'd never want to be trapped together for good with her. And his 'contract' was too unbalanced. He was offering a ring and room in his penthouse…and what did she bring to the party? Her overly efficient womb.

'You're offering all this…paying for so much,' she said awkwardly. 'It doesn't seem fair. What do you get out of it?'

His expression smouldered. 'I get what I want.'

Something heavy shifted within her. That low drag deep in her belly that pulled her towards him. But he meant the baby, right?

'Ettie.' That low, irresistible growl sounded.

'Yes.' It whispered out before she'd even thought it.

He was the one who moved, walking towards her until there was too little space between them. 'Let's go and get your things from your flat.' His voice was husky.

She couldn't move.

'Ettie…' He put his hand on her waist. The amber lights glowed in his deep brown eyes. But he didn't smile. He looked edgier than ever as he applied pressure and pulled her against him until she was in no doubt of his physical response to her.

'Will this be…part of the contract?' She flung her chin up, determined to hold her own with him. Because if she couldn't do that now, she had no chance of keeping him in check.

Something flashed in his eyes. 'I'll be faithful to you and I expect the same in return. But I'm not going to demand sexual favours. There won't be a clause detailing a minimum number of intimacies each week.'

She opened her mouth, shocked at the suggestion. At the appallingly hot response of her treacherous body to such a requirement.

'If anything happens, it's up to us in that moment. Just like normal,' he said. 'No expectations, no repercussions…regardless of what we do in private.'

No repercussions? It was so ironic, but she couldn't laugh. Right now she couldn't even breathe.

He ran his hand down her spine, coming to rest his palm on the curve of her hip. 'Maybe we should stop negotiating...'

Her body melted. He was seducing her into saying yes. And she knew he could, so easily. Abruptly she pulled out from his hold. 'Maybe you don't try to distract me like that.'

'Maybe that kind of distraction would be good for you,' he countered with a small smile.

Sensation rippled down her spine. 'Maybe we should just go and get my stuff.'

She heard his low laugh as she walked away. She realised too late that he'd manipulated her into doing what he wanted. He'd easily played her...because he knew she was weak with want for him still. She screwed her eyes shut; that was *so* mortifying. Echoes of her ex-fiancé's callousness circled in her head—building her demons of insecurity. She *hated* her inexperience.

'Come on, *glykia mou*. Let's get moving.'

'What does it mean?' she asked. 'That expression?'

Another flicker of a smile curved his lips. 'My sweet.'

'You think that's going to get you extra points?' she asked tartly. But she was breathless beneath the weak sarcasm. It was *really* unfair of him because he didn't mean it.

'I think it's only a matter of time,' he murmured wryly. 'And I think you know it as well as I do.'

'You weren't interested in a repeat,' she said stiffly.

'Because you shut me down.' He shot her an astounded look. 'I was respecting *your* wishes.' And he didn't look all that happy about it.

Her heart thundered. He'd thought she'd shut him down? 'And now?'

'All bets are off.'

Craving curled through her body. Intense, shocking, explicit want. It was desire for contact, right? Physical closeness because she felt alone. It was just an instinctive, basic need that she was determined to suppress.

'The situation is what it is, Ettie,' he added. 'We might as well make the most of it.'

'And in your world "making the most of it" is us sleeping together again?' she jeered bitterly.

'We do it pretty well.'

Pretty well? Great. For him it had been just as average as she'd feared and he was just using *her* weakness for him to get what he wanted.

He suddenly chuckled. 'Oh, Ettie, you're so transparent.'

Before she could argue he turned her to face him and brushed his lips over hers in the lightest whisper of a kiss. Her breathing faltered—all that tantalising promise was only a breath away. But he didn't mean any of it.

'It's not fair of you to tease me this way.' She valiantly defended her heart when he lifted his head from hers.

Because he knew, didn't he, just how overwhelmed she was by his sensuality?

But at her words he stilled. A second after the lift

door opened, she found herself with her back against the wall of the lift and he was right there in front of her. Hot, fierce fury unfurled deep and low in her belly at the smoking expression in his eyes.

'I'm not teasing,' he muttered.

Leon slammed his mouth over hers—determined to draw out her spark even if it was only because she was aggravated with him. He wanted her fire. He kissed her hard and deep, plundering her softness with a flick of his tongue. The flare within her was instant. Her hunger took him by surprise and unleashed his own. Hell, he'd wanted this and he'd been too long denied. He curled her arms around his neck so he could haul her closer and grind her against the wall. Her fingers twisted and locked in his hair.

The heady relief at having her in his arms again contrasted with the burning desire tightening his body to the point of pain. He was angry she'd held him at bay when she so clearly craved his touch the way he ached for hers. Now he was mad with her. Now he wanted to torment her. To please her.

She moaned as he cupped her breast with a firm, greedy hand. Her nipple strained against her shirt. Her fingers tightened in his hair. She was so hot he lost his head completely, rushing straight back into that insane intensity of all-consuming lust. He'd suffered weeks of being without this. He didn't know how he'd stood it.

A bell pinged somewhere in the distance. It took him a moment to realise that the lift door had slid open.

'Oh, excuse me.'

Leon froze and glanced down at Ettie, amused to see her turn bright pink. She hurriedly disentangled her fingers from his hair and craned her head to see who it was talking.

It turned out the lift hadn't stopped at the basement. He hadn't even had the brains to push the damn buttons in his haste to touch her. The lift had been summoned by another resident. As a result it had stopped halfway down the building and right now Autumn Welby was staring at them with frank fascination.

'I'll wait for the lift to return. Nice to see you're back, Ettie,' she said breezily. 'I'm so glad you're feeling better.'

Leon glanced again at Ettie, but now she'd gone pale. He tightened one arm around her waist and reached out with the other to push the button on the lift.

'Ettie won't be back on the concierge desk for the foreseeable future,' he said briskly, sending Autumn a dismissive smile.

'Oh.' Autumn nodded. 'Lovely for you, terrible for me.'

The lift doors slid shut again and he looked back into Ettie's face to see nothing but fury.

'For the foreseeable future?' she repeated in a frigid voice. 'Just like that, Leon?'

Yeah, just like that. He wasn't about to apologise and he didn't have the brain to explain it all just yet.

She extricated herself from his arm and folded her

own across her chest, all but tapping her foot as the lift swept down to the basement.

'Everyone will know now.' She threw him an appalled look as she stomped out into the garage. 'Everyone will know in minutes.'

'Ettie, we're getting married. You're having my baby.' He followed her slowly, determined to remain calm and get his head around her response to that kiss. 'They're going to find out some time anyway; it might as well be now.'

She drew herself up short and whirled to face him. 'But it's so early…'

A horrible thought hit. Was she worried about miscarrying the baby? Was that even a possibility? A surge of protectiveness—and self-condemnation—welled in him. He shouldn't be pawing her when she needed rest.

'Everything will be fine.' He pushed past the hoarseness in his voice and led her to his roadster. He didn't want his driver for this ride. He needed his own hands on the wheel. 'You're fit, healthy, strong.'

And so damn beautiful that all he wanted to do was scoop her into his arms, toss her onto the nearest bed and pick up where they'd left off before they'd been so brutally interrupted. But he couldn't exhaust her with his selfish lust. He had to put both her and the baby ahead of his own desire. Ettie needed certainty and security. She had too many worries, too many responsibilities. But he'd lift them from her. And while lust might not last, it would get them through this phase until they settled into a long-term arrangement.

He could provide her with a lifestyle she'd only ever dreamed about. She'd never have to worry about paying for her own groceries or heating again. She didn't have to scrimp and save for her sister's education. She could care for their baby and breathe easily for the rest of her life. Those key points she could never argue against and never beat. He had this situation won and she knew it.

'You'll have to get another car.' She glanced at the Italian two-seater.

He nodded.

'What about Ophelia's holidays?'

'I have plenty of space.' He didn't tell her he meant his London home. They weren't staying at Cavendish House another night. She was too uncomfortable and he understood that. They needed privacy. She needed the space to let go of her inhibitions—to scream his name as she came.

Cool it, Romeo. He mocked himself. She was exhausted and overwhelmed and the last thing she needed was him making physical demands on her. He'd won already. He could wait a little longer.

CHAPTER SEVEN

IT TOOK ETTIE only five minutes later to fill a small case with clothes and a few very personal effects from her flat. She went to fetch her coat from where it hung over the back of a chair.

'Leave it,' he said. 'We'll get you a new one.'

She stiffened, saddened that he'd noticed how worn it was. She cast a last glance around the room. How was it possible that such a tiny apartment could feel so empty? She'd helped her sister learn to read here. She'd made Ophelia's lunches and cleaned her uniforms. For so long it had been the two of them against the world...

And she wasn't telling Ophelia about this yet. Not until she'd got control of everything—mostly her emotions.

'I'll get the rest of your things boxed up; don't worry about any of it.'

Don't worry?

Her mother had fallen for the wrong man more than once. Ettie had made an almighty mistake putting her faith in a guy already... But maybe Leon's way was right? Maybe it was as simple as writing up the list—the pros and the cons and being cool-headed about it.

He wanted the baby. She came with it. So he'd keep her happy to keep her onside—give her a home, help support her sister. He might even have sex with her if she played her cards right. But even that for him wasn't *emotional*. It was a relaxant—a satisfying physical release. An added bonus to the deal they'd made.

Maybe it could be just fun for her too? Maybe she could be more like Leon? He seemed to have it so completely together...

The irony was that everything had been pretty fine—better than it had in ages actually. She'd been making it work in this final stretch of Ophelia's schooling. But now it felt as if her life had fragmented and all the elements were slipping from her control. She was furious with herself. But she couldn't quite regret it completely.

She watched Leon drive them back into the heart of London. He seemed to enjoy controlling the powerful machine. He appeared as calm as ever. Certain of his place in the world and the decisions he made. It was as if his handsome face had been carved from marble by a master craftsman. Expressionless. Emotionless, he'd locked back into business focus easily. So he really had only been teasing moments ago, while she'd been almost *desperate* for his touch. Now she shivered with a horrible fear she was going to feel even more alone living in his apartment.

'Where are we going?' She sat up and twisted

to read the road sign. 'We just went past Cavendish House.'

'We're going home.'

'The penthouse there is your home.'

'No, that's where I was staying for a few weeks while I studied my new investment. *This* is my home.'

They'd turned into a quiet side street in the heart of Mayfair. Her heart ceased beating. It wasn't an apartment in a building, but the *whole* building. She'd known he was wealthy, but this wasn't a millionaire's penthouse; this property was worth multi-multi-millions—a billionaire's mansion in one of the most expensive streets on the planet.

'How many bedrooms?' she muttered.

'Only six.' He walked ahead of her. 'Four bathrooms.'

Oh, was that all? She shook her head after him as he led the way. There was a gleaming kitchen—light, airy, equipped with appliances Ettie wouldn't know how to turn on…

'There's a catering kitchen and staff quarters downstairs.'

She blinked. 'You have a lot of staff?'

'I have a housekeeper; she doesn't live on site but she comes every other day. She'll prep food for us if we want. My executive assistant sometimes uses it if we're working late on a deal.'

'Oh?' She tried not to imagine his beautiful assistant. 'I expect she's very efficient.'

Leon sent her a sideways, all too knowing look. 'He is.'

Ettie stared, overwhelmed by the trio of reception

rooms. The home gym and pool and cinema room almost gave her conniptions. It was all beautifully furnished in muted greys and neutrals, with pops of colour—shades of blue in a few rooms, green in another. The curved wrought-iron balustrade of the staircase revealed snippets of the delights of each level. There were both polished wooden floors and plush carpets, and the light fittings sparkled like works of art themselves…speaking of which, striking paintings adorned the walls. The bathrooms were lined with vast marble and gleaming chrome…the entire house was a simply exquisite, designer's wet dream.

Yeah, he'd really been slumming it at Cavendish House. She'd thought *that* was exclusive, but this was a whole new level of luxury.

'Why did you buy it?' she asked out of complete curiosity. What did he need such a big home for?

He looked surprised by her question. 'I liked it.' He glanced around the recreation room. 'Don't you like it?'

She'd have to be mad not to adore it. She thought of the inviting crystal-clear blue of his indoor pool and the spa alongside it. 'You use the beauty treatment room often?'

Grinning, he shook his head. 'No, nor the bar and home cinema much either. You're welcome to it all, of course; this is your home now.'

She didn't think she'd ever feel at home in such an immaculate, luxurious space. It seemed every item in it was unique and priceless.

'Where are the bedrooms?'

He led her up the curving staircase. 'There are a couple of bedrooms on each of these floors. The study up on the top floor opens onto a rooftop terrace; it's nice on sunny days. But this is my room.'

His bedroom alone was larger than her entire flat. An enormous bed was the centrepiece, but the room was large enough to hold a sofa and an armchair as well as a beautiful wooden cabinet. A wide doorway offered a glimpse of the gleaming marble and black finish of his bathroom.

She cleared her throat. 'Which is my room?'

He sent her a glinting look. 'If you don't want to be in mine, you can choose any of the others. Though I'd prefer it if you were on the same floor as me. For later in the pregnancy.'

No, she did not want to be in his room, or even on his *floor*. He wasn't having everything his own way.

Ettie snatched up her bag and marched to the bedroom furthest from his, knowing damn well she was spiting herself as much as him in this small act of defiance.

'I'm going to run a couple of errands,' he said coolly, following her to the room she chose. 'I'll be back in an hour or so. You take your time and settle in.'

'Okay,' she said.

'Fancy anything in particular to eat?'

She shook her head. 'Whatever you think will be nice.'

He nodded and left.

It took only a moment for Ettie to hang her few clothes—they really didn't suit the designer walk-in wardrobe. With a rueful grimace, she walked around the house again—taking in more details now Leon wasn't here to distract her. It really was incredible. It even had its own garden, which in this space-at-a-premium part of London was almost unheard-of. The whole place was impeccably maintained—that housekeeper clearly had fun keeping it pristine and photo-spread-worthy, with perfectly folded towels at the ready and vases of fresh flowers to give the place vibrancy. All this for one guy?

He came from a completely different world to hers.

But what struck her even more was the lack of anything particularly personal of Leon's on display. There were no family photos, or holiday snaps. The only vaguely personal images were some arty black and white shots of some buildings—buildings he owned, including this one. It seemed his property empire was everything he cared about.

She returned to the bedroom she'd chosen and walked into the stunning white and grey marble bathroom. She simply couldn't resist that deep-set bath. Not when there was that selection of French perfumed soaps and salts to add to it. Not when she needed to relax so badly. A few minutes later she sank into the gloriously scented, warm depths.

But her raging thoughts wouldn't quieten. That was impossible when her world had been totally turned upside down. Leon Kariakis was insisting they marry. Offering a *contract,* not his heart. But she was going to be okay with that because she was *not* going to make the mistakes of her own past, or of her mother's. She was going to learn from Leon—be businesslike and efficient.

She slipped lower, appreciating the silken slide of the water on her bare skin, and her mind wandered to less *businesslike* imaginings. This bath was definitely built big enough for two.

All thoughts of efficiency fled as sexual frustration suddenly flared. Why hadn't he touched her again since they were interrupted in that lift? That kiss had been incendiary and she ached for more. The nausea that had plagued her for days had dissipated as arousal replaced it. She wanted him to send her into that place where thoughts couldn't impinge, where there was only feeling and pleasure and so much *touch*...

'Ettie?'

She almost jumped right out of the bath.

'Sorry, I won't be a minute,' she gasped. 'I'm just in the bath.'

There was a moment's silence on the other side of the door. 'You must be hungry.' He sounded a little huskier.

Absolutely. But not for what he meant. 'Sure. I won't be long.'

She levered herself out of the bath, wrapped her body in one of the enormous plush towels and quickly dressed.

He was waiting for her in the kitchen. 'I got this for you,' he said without preamble, pushing a small box across the counter to her.

Ettie's heart stopped. Reluctantly, but unable to refuse, she opened the box. She blinked a couple of times, almost blinded. 'Where'd you get it from?'

'Christmas cracker, where do you think?'

'You bought it?'

'Well, I didn't steal it.' He rolled his eyes.

She didn't ask if it was synthetic. She didn't want to give him another chance to look smug.

'You can't just buy what you want,' she muttered, her resistance to him building in a wave of heat and fury. Because it was such a beautiful ring and there was that weak, romantic, *foolish* part of her that would've loved to be given this in another time, another circumstance, with other words... 'You can't buy me,' she added ferociously.

'I know that,' he said softly. 'If there's anyone who knows money can't buy happiness, it's me.'

His reply struck her silent. Unexpected and revealing—had he not been happy? When? She waited, willing him to say more. Instead she watched that expressionless veil slide across the flare in his eyes.

'Just put it on, Ettie.'

It was a flawless square-cut emerald set in a platinum band. A large diamond sat either side of the pale green stone. Simple yet sublime, and so very stunning.

She stalled for time because she was shaking inside. She'd never touched anything like it in her life.

'You often go out to get takeaways and come back with precious jewels?'

'Every Wednesday. You can set your watch by me.'

Smart Alec. 'I thought this was business.'

'It's personal business.' But there was a glint flicking in his eyes again. 'And it is straightforward.'

How could it be? He didn't think this was complicated?

Was this really just another acquisition for him—a fiancée and a baby? He was so in control and unconcerned and capable. Didn't he feel fear? Didn't he feel anything? Was he really as emotionless as he appeared?

'Stop overthinking. It'll work out.' He walked around the counter, took the ring out of the box and reached out to hold her cold hand. 'For the baby, okay? You want your child to have two actively involved parents. Here you go. A united front. A team, Ettie.'

She sent him a baleful look. She did want that, very much. Because it was what she hadn't had and he knew it. He was counting on that as he slid the ring down.

But people co-parented the world over with perfectly amicable arrangements and weren't married or even engaged. They made it work. There was no reason why she and Leon couldn't work out something just as successful.

Except his argument for marriage was compelling. She too wanted her child to have the security Leon was offering. And she'd nailed being practical

at work, so why couldn't she apply the same to her
personal life?

Intuition sent a tinge of unease down her spine.
The problem was *his* magnetism. He only needed to
stand this close, to hold her hand like this, and her
heart was racing, sending excitement through every
vein, to every cell. Ettie could fall far and fast—make
the mistake of believing that, rather than being his
"for the practicalities" fiancée, she was his match for
real. And that wasn't fair on him. Or on her. Because
the same was so not happening for him. He was *only*
about the practicalities.

So she had to focus on the same. Keep her guard
up, warn off her weak, blind heart.

She hauled together all her emotional strength and
pulled her hand from his, tore her gaze from his.
She'd accept this for what it was.

She smiled down at the ring. 'It's beautiful, thank
you.' Then she turned, desperately commenting on
the first thing she saw. 'I didn't know you already
had a dog.' She was determined to make things easy
and casual between them.

Blinking, he sent her a mystified look.

'The dog bowl on the bench behind you?'

'Oh?' His eyebrows snapped down, forming a
frown. 'I ordered those when I thought that Toby
might stay.'

Really?

'I'm sorry I said yes to that resident taking him
without talking to you first,' she muttered thought-
fully. The sense she'd wronged him somehow in mak-

ing that choice had been nagging her for these last couple of days.

'Don't apologise; it was best for the dog,' he said crisply.

So he hadn't really wanted him? But she'd sent Toby to that other resident the very next day, so Leon had been super-quick off the mark getting in bowls for him. But that was just his hyper-efficiency, wasn't it? Just as he'd convinced her to agree to marrying him and ensconced her in his home within two hours of learning she was pregnant. It was how he was a billionaire before thirty. Leon Kariakis got stuff done with single-minded, ruthless efficiency and there was nothing emotional about it.

Yet she couldn't look away from him—aware once more of that simmering intensity that his stillness masked. He'd loosened his tie and his shirtsleeves were rolled back and a tuft of hair was still ruffled. She suspected it was from when she'd run her fingers through his hair in the lift earlier. Did he know how tormenting he was?

'You're feeling better.' He changed the subject.

Yes. With every step closer she was to him unfortunately. And she was incredibly curious. He wasn't just a closed book. He was padlocked-and-sealed-in-an-underground-vault private. But they were having a baby together. Getting married. Even in business arrangements, people did due diligence, didn't they? Maybe if she offered information first—broke the ice—he might feel a gentle obligation to reciprocate?

'My father wasn't there for me. Ever,' she said quietly.

He paused and glanced at her.

'So thank you for wanting to stick around.'

He tensed. 'I'm not like him.'

'I know.' The guy was already a better father than what her own had been and what Ophelia's had been by the simple fact he was actually interested. 'My mother got her heart broken a couple of times. It hurt her badly.' She was quiet a moment before summoning courage. 'What about your parents?'

'Absent, mostly.'

Really? She was surprised. 'Didn't they turn up to sports day?'

'No. Are you ready to eat? You must be hungry.'

She frowned, irritated that he'd shut that conversation down so quickly. 'We can't just…start living together and being engaged. We need to get to know each other, Leon.'

He blinked at her again. 'What do you want to know?'

'I don't know. Anything.' Everything. She glanced at those empty bowls on the far bench. 'Did you have a dog when you were a kid?'

'No.' To her amazement his expression became like blank granite. 'Come on, dinner is on the table.'

'Which one?' she asked tartly.

Leon knew he'd been abrupt, but some things she didn't need to know. Life was for living in *now*, not remembering the miseries of the past. He tried to ignore the prickling at the base of his spine. He was satisfied she was in his house finally, yet he was unbearably aware of her in his space. The mansion was large but her presence seemed to permeate every inch...the scent of her, the soft sounds as she moved about.

He'd had to get out just to clear his head. Sort out the ring as consideration for the contract. Decide on dinner. Check in with his assistant and ensure everything at the office was under control...but he'd listened with only half-concentration and in the end he'd not been able to get back fast enough to check on her.

Stupid to be so concerned. He knew emotions weakened a man—muddying the mind and making decision-making difficult. Isolation and independence brought clarity. There were mergers and acquisitions, splits and divisions, and this was just another. It should be simple.

'Oh.'

He suppressed a chuckle as Ettie came to a halt at the entrance to the formal dining room.

'When did you do this?' She gaped at the table laden with dishes.

'It was delivered while you were in the bath.'

She gazed from the table to the discreet trolley in the corner. 'It's from a restaurant.'

Yeah, as concierge to an exclusive apartment building, she knew how it worked. He paid, the staff delivered. And it was worth it for the privacy.

She lifted the silver cover of the nearest dish and her eyebrows lifted. 'Do you only dine from award-winning restaurants?'

He took a seat and stared at her with all the lazy arrogance he could muster. 'I like savouring perfection,' he drawled.

She rolled her eyes and he laughed in delight.

'You asked for it,' he ribbed her. 'You think I'm pompous? I can eat a wrap on the street from a food van like anyone else, but tonight I want to sit in comfort and privacy and let *all* my senses feast.' He sent her a meaningful look. 'I have a pretty companion to ogle. Besides which, you're tired and you need a decent meal.'

And frankly, her enjoyment of decent food increased his own pleasure in it.

She sighed and sank into the chair opposite his. 'You're so used to doing everything your own way, aren't you?'

'Isn't everyone?'

She laughed aloud, a bubble of genuine amusement. 'The fate of the only child,' she teased. 'You've never had to learn to compromise.'

He tried to smile but his mouth had swiftly dried. It wasn't her fault. She simply didn't know.

'You're very serious,' she continued her judgement. 'Hard-working.'

'It's how I became successful.' He tried not to sound like a stiff-necked ass, but it was true.

'So,' she angled her head to study him, that teasing light brightening her eyes even more, 'not a wild playboy…at least not publicly. You were never the spoilt heir to a fortune who fritters it all away on women and wine and destructive vices…'

'No, that's not me.'

'But why not?' She seemed quite fascinated. 'It's the trap lots of people in your position fall into, isn't it? Stories like that fill the news... Playboy heirs. Dissolute, depraved, who end up broke—'

'Or dying of an overdose; I get the picture,' he finished coldly. 'I guess that's not the way I was raised.'

'So how were you raised?'

He eyed her across the table and she met his censuring look with a radiant smile of utter innocence. Yeah, she knew what she was doing and he knew she wasn't about to let up.

'Strictly,' he muttered.

'You said they were absent.' She looked thoughtful. 'Do you see them now?'

He didn't think of his parents much and he certainly never discussed them. Why would he? But he had to give her something—she was like a dog with a bone. The bald facts would do. 'We have dinner once every six months. It's scheduled—the full year in advance. We discuss returns, hotel occupancy rates, the stock market.'

Her eyes widened. 'Twice a year?'

'Yes.'

'And that's it?'

'Yes.' He could see her mind working overtime.

'Do you ever take a date?'

'Never. It's an obligation on both sides. They never doubted I would do anything other than succeed. And they ensured I was never spoiled by the wealth I was born into.'

He pointedly stabbed a chunk of steak and shoved it into his mouth. That was enough, surely? She was more curious than a barn full of cats. And the meat tasted like sawdust and glue. He made it go down with a hard swallow. 'Look, I know you're worried about how little we know of each other, but it isn't something that can be forced, or hurried,' he said, closing off the conversation. 'Time will take care of it.'

She still looked thoughtful. And utterly unconvinced. 'Most people wouldn't work as hard as you if they didn't have to.'

'Why not? Don't we all need a purpose? A sense of dignity from a job well done? What makes you think I wouldn't need that too?'

'But to be so driven... When is it enough?' She gestured at the furnishings in the large room. 'What is it you have to prove?'

'I don't need to prove anything,' he growled. 'Perhaps it's just that the goalposts shift. I make a plan to achieve one thing, when it's knocked off I feel like a challenge for something more. Isn't that human nature?'

A shadow crossed her eyes. 'So you're never satisfied with what you have?'

His chest tightened and he laughed and groaned at the same time because her effervescent curiosity was going to be the death of him. But she was irresistible. It was that manner that made her so popular with the residents at Cavendish House. She made you feel like you could confide everything in her and she'd sort it all out for you. 'I'm satisfied,' he growled. 'I just want *more*.'

Right now he was greedy for *her*. She was wearing a thin old T-shirt and jeans that hung a little loose. But she was still flushed from that bath and her skin looked luminous and silky soft. She smelled tantalising and her hair was a wild, damp mess down her back and he just wanted to thrust his hands into the gorgeous length of it and bind her close beneath him.

'I'll tell you something, Ettie,' he said bluntly, shoving those X-rated thoughts to the back of his mind, 'when you come from a background like mine, you swiftly learn that people only stick around because they want something from you.'

She perked up. 'Is that true, really?' She looked at him keenly, a teasing smile flicking at her mouth. 'Aren't there any uncomplicated, nice people out there who just want to be friends?'

He couldn't help but laugh. 'Perhaps I'm too prejudiced to be able to spot them.' He leaned closer and called her out on it. 'Even you wanted something from me.'

'But you wanted the same thing from me.' She wagged a finger at him. 'So that makes us even.'

'I'm as bad as you?' he asked in mock-outrage.

'Possibly worse. Because you took advantage of everything you have to seduce me.'

'And you didn't?' He scoffed. 'With your wild ponytail and passionate eyes?'

'My what?' She looked astounded.

'All the emotions.' He pointed to her eyes, suddenly quite serious. 'Here.'

'What are my eyes expressing now?' she asked, still but breathless.

He stared at her intently—searching those beautifully clear eyes for the signal he'd wanted for so long. And then it was there.

'Your desire for me to take you to bed.' He simply snapped. He didn't want to think any more. Didn't want to try to solve unworkable problems. Damn well didn't want to talk around the issues or, heaven forbid, his freaking past. He didn't want to think of her being hurt by some jerk and her mum dying and leaving her to raise her sister alone. He wanted to relax, damn it. Eat good food and kiss the beautiful woman in front of him over every inch of her delectable body until she arched and begged him to finish her hard and fast. Everything else be blowed.

Her mouth opened, then shut and he could see her deciding how to handle her reply.

'Wow. Impressive.' But her sass was all bluff because what he'd said was true.

He clocked her rising colour, her quickening breath, her widening eyes. And he really didn't want to talk any more. Talking wasn't anywhere near as effective as action. He'd thought he should back off, especially after she'd been so mortified about that woman catching them in the lift. But they needed to clear the air of this tension that kept building. There was only here and now. Together they'd find oblivion.

He pushed back from the table and stalked around

to where she now sat bolt upright. He grabbed her hand and tugged her to her feet.

She thought he'd seduced her that night? That was nothing on what he was about to do. He wasn't waiting. He wasn't taking this slow. He wanted her beneath him, about him. He craved the welcome of her soft heat. He pulled her against his body and gazed into her green eyes. For a moment it was as if they'd romped back to that first night—soft laughter, whispered desire, sensual freedom. It didn't need to be anything more than that.

But there was no time for whispered words and soft laughter tonight. His need was too raw. He kissed her, and in that moment it was all over.

Unrestrained, ruthless, he stripped her bare right there in the formal dining room, boldly touching every spot he revealed. The emerald and diamond ring caught the light, sending small, sparking chinks of light onto the ceiling. His pleasure intensified at seeing her wearing it—the time-worn signal that she was taken. For a second he stilled, paralysed by the sudden ferocious anticipation of seeing her belly swell with her pregnancy over the coming months. She'd be softened and ripe with his child. His mark. He wanted to mark her all over—suddenly possessed by a primal, appalling need to stamp her as his. And he gave way to it in that instant, curling his arm around her waist to lift her up and carry her to his bed.

He wasn't making her come in five different ways before filling her this time. He wasn't letting her come at all. Not until she was unable to bear it a second longer. Not until she begged for mercy. Not until they were both at the end of their sanity. In the cage of his arms he caressed her, alternating with licks, love bites, kisses—he teased and tasted every inch of her glorious body. She was pregnant. She was hot. And she was his.

He laughed roughly as she moaned, her hips circling, her hands seeking to touch him too. He suffered the tormenting slide of her fingertips, the delight of her hard grip, and moved to retaliate. He relished the way her muscles quivered under his onslaught. But nothing pleased him more than the look of hunger in her eyes. She was as willing, as craving, as he.

'Leon, please. *Please.*'

He paused above her, soaking in the moment he'd been aching for.

'Why have you stopped?' she asked, her expression edged with desperation.

'I don't want this over too soon,' he answered with rough honesty.

'I've wanted this for weeks,' she moaned. 'So much.'

Satisfaction and frustration split him. Fire and fury. 'Then why did you deny us?' Why had she put up those barriers? He was making her pay for that. '*Why* did you resist?'

How had she? But he couldn't wait for her answer—the demand of his own body, his own need, was too strong. She moaned in soft, earthy surrender as he thrust hard, fiercely claiming his possession. He arched, his eyes closing as pleasure sent sharp bursts down his back. His body tightened more, wanted more—deeper, harder, for *longer*. But she lost it beneath him, about him, crying out as her sweet body was wracked with the feral convulsions of one hell of an orgasm. But this wasn't over yet. He simply *refused* to let it be over yet. So he held still, his will stretched to the point of pain.

'Leon, it's so intense,' she gasped. 'So intense.'

'All the more reason to embrace it,' he growled, still furious with her for making them wait all these weeks.

'Please,' she begged, breathless and twisting and fierce beneath him. 'Please, Leon.'

It was as much a desperate plea as a forceful command. And now he could do nothing but surrender to both. He felt torn in two by the fierce, unrelenting urges to both master and worship her body.

'Ettie,' he growled. Demanding. Devoted.

The give and take, the push and pull was mirrored in his hard thrusts, in the buck of her fiery hips. He roared as his shy lover responded with that fight. She was that desperate for him. Which he adored because he couldn't get enough of her either. She made him both weak and strong. He was almost rendered unconscious by the ferocity of the pleasure as he pushed her to climax again. Yet her scream was silent, her body so taut with tension, shaking with intense delight, it couldn't render it vocally. The sight of her in that moment stopped his heart. His release came, instant and savage and so intense he all but blacked out.

When he returned to reality and summoned the energy to lift his head, he was horrified to find her face pale, her eyes simply huge and—glistening with tears?

'Are you okay?' he asked warily. Guilt hit him anew.

She was *exhausted* and he'd just subjected her to the roughest of rides. 'Sleep.' He drew the coverings over her, partly to hide the resurgence of his own desire, impossible as it ought to have been. He'd wanted her too much for too long. But surely he could wait until tomorrow before having her again?

Shadows crept into her beautiful, clear eyes. 'I can go back to my room.'

An ice-cold storm brewed in his belly. 'You want that?'

She licked her lips and glanced away from him. 'If that's what you'd prefer.'

Of course he wouldn't. 'What's going on, Ettie? Was I too rough?'

'No.' She wiped her eyes and turned away.

Not good enough. He turned her back towards him and gazed into her eyes. 'Then what?'

Her colour mounted and she seemed to be holding her breath. 'That other night you couldn't seem to get enough…but if you don't really want me any more, we don't have to…'

If he didn't really want her?

'Ettie,' he huffed out a relieved laugh, 'I thought you were exhausted. I didn't want to be too demanding…' He lost his train of thought as he saw the shadows shift to smoke in her eyes. '*Glykia mou.*'

'Sorry,' she muttered, colour flooding her face.

'Why?' He pulled her closer. 'I'm not sorry that my new fiancée is a nymphomaniac.'

He laughed at her gasp of outrage and thrust back the coverings so he could satisfy his need to see her naked beauty all over again.

'We *do* have to, Ettie.' He bent over her uncompromisingly. 'We damned well do.'

He angled her so he could see right into her eyes as he swept his hands over her soft curves and watched the ebb and flow of her tension. To his relief and pleasure, her smile returned. A more feminine, more feline one than he'd ever seen on her. He growled and surged into her—slower this time, tormenting them both to the point of madness. And it was utter bliss.

'I didn't know it could be this much fun.' She almost laughed a long while later.

Fun? Had she thought that was *fun*?

He'd thought it was devastating. But he cleared his throat and pulled his brain back from its fanciful, post-orgasmic superlatives. 'It's supposed to be fun.' And now he was looking, he couldn't tear his eyes from the satisfied glow enveloping her. 'You look better than you have in days.'

'I feel better.' Her cheeks were rosy and there was a relaxed softness in her expression. She was stunning.

But he cocked his head and aimed to tease them both back to lightness. 'Orgasms for medicinal purposes?'

'Who knew, right?' She giggled.

'What happened with your ex?' The question just

slipped out at that most appalling moment. He hadn't meant to ask it—not ever. But the idea that she'd cared for another man enough to want to marry him had grated on his deepest-set nerves. What had been so special about the jerk? Why had he let her go?

Leon gritted his teeth—why did he even want to know? But he did. Desperately.

Ettie was too quiet. He rolled to his side and propped his head up on his hand, studying the return of those shadows. They flickered across her face— resistance, sadness. He hated that some guy had hurt her. He didn't mean to hurt her more by asking about it now. Were the memories that painful? Had the bastard mattered so much she could barely bring herself to speak about him?

'He jilted me just before our wedding,' she finally answered.

'At the altar?' His skin tightened.

'Almost.' She seemed to shrink deeper into the mattress. 'His family had arrived. My friends. Ophelia was so excited about being bridesmaid…it was so humiliating…'

'Why did he do it? Was there someone else?' He couldn't fathom it. What man wouldn't want Ettie in his life? She was sexy, she was funny, she was sweet.

She looked away from him.

'We hadn't been intimate,' she said huskily. 'I'd wanted to wait.'

Leon's brain malfunctioned for a moment. *Not intimate? Wait?* 'You hadn't been intimate at all?'

She shook her head. 'We'd kissed but…' She shrivelled lower into the mattress and tugged the sheet higher. 'I wanted to wait.'

'For your wedding night?' He stilled as a bubble of something hot and fierce and frankly savage bubbled in his gut. That she'd wanted to do that—gift the guy her virginity—made his innards twist.

'I know, it's quaint, right?' She wouldn't look at him.

He shook his head. 'Sweet,' he corrected gruffly.

'I should have known it wasn't right.'

'What do you mean?'

'It wasn't hard for me to want to wait.' She lowered her chin and all but talked into the sheet covering her. 'I thought I had a low sex drive. That it was just me.'

His eyes widened. The woman didn't have a low sex drive. She was the hottest, most insatiable lover of his life. 'But your fiancé didn't want to wait any more?'

'He said it was so close to the wedding…that we should.'

He'd applied pressure and manipulated her innate desire to please. Leon tensed. 'And how was it?'

Her face burned red again. 'He didn't stick around for the wedding, so I guess it wasn't that good.'

So it had been just the once? He had to snap his mouth to keep his jaw from hitting the floor. 'And there's been no one since?'

Her blush built to beetroot, making it easy to read the deep embarrassment and insecurity all over her expressive face. She thought she wasn't sexy, that she didn't know what she was doing. That she'd not been able to satisfy her selfish ass of a fiancé. So there'd been that one let-down of an experience followed by appalling betrayal and rejection after.

And then there'd been him.

'That's why I was so reckless when you… It was so different…' She fell silent, that mottled rosy pink slowly washed from her skin.

He was savagely proud it had been so *different*. 'Poor Ettie. You finally let go enough to have some fun, and then—'

'I end up pregnant,' she mumbled.

One night. Massive consequences. It wasn't exactly fair.

'I guess mindless, meaningless, fantastic sex just isn't for me,' she attempted to joke.

'No, it is,' he replied, utterly serious. 'It just needs to be with me.'

She flushed deeper and her smile faded. 'Is it good for you?'

Was she seriously worried about that? He couldn't keep his hands off her. But that jerk had hurt her, striking an insecurity within.

'There's nothing wrong with you,' he whispered. 'Nothing wrong with what you do, how you respond…' He ripped back the sheet from them both. 'Look at what you do to me.'

She turned her face away but he tenderly cupped her chin and made her look. And then he kissed her— long, deep and lush—and felt that fire between them crackle.

'He was a jerk, Ettie,' Leon muttered, filled with protectiveness.

'He was. I just wanted to please him.'

He hated the bastard who'd had no idea of the treasure he'd had in his hands. He hated the damage he'd done to her. But he had to ease up on releasing that rage. She was more vulnerable than her ultra-efficient, all-smiling concierge persona revealed. 'You left school early and had to work?' He talked, trying to contain his anger and ease the tension gripping his muscles.

'Initially I left because Mum got sick. I needed to care for her and Ophelia.'

But she'd been a kid herself—just a teen. He hadn't wanted to listen earlier, but now he wanted to know everything. 'There was no one else?'

'She was young when she got pregnant with me. She was estranged from her parents—I never had a relationship with them or my father. Ophelia was the result of another doomed-to-failure fling. She'd wanted it to work out with him…'

'But that didn't happen either.'

She shook her head. 'Relationships never worked out for her.'

A chill swept over his skin. 'And you held off having boyfriends.'

'I was too busy to meet anyone,' she said softly.

'No,' he contradicted her. 'You shied away from them.' He understood why—she'd seen her mother's heartache and it had put her off. She'd seen the consequences—she'd lived them. He couldn't resist asking the question that burned in his gut. 'What did he give you that others didn't?' Why had she said yes to that guy?

'I met him not long after Mum died. It was very quick and I was vulnerable, I guess. He flattered me. He made me think I was special.'

Leon hardened inside. 'So he should've done—he was your boyfriend.'

'I wanted someone to love me. I thought he did. But he didn't.'

Leon didn't believe in love. He didn't believe anyone had it—they had habits and pleasant arrangements. But he could offer Ettie loyalty. 'I'll never betray you like that.'

She looked at him sombrely. Didn't she trust him yet?

'Can we always be honest with each other?' she asked softly. 'Like you said, we're not talking stardust and promises. Don't flatter me. Don't try to soften any blows. Let's just be grounded and honest.'

That fierce savagery clawed at his insides and he finally lost his grip on it. 'Okay, here's some honesty for you: I crave your body, Ettie. I've dreamed about having you again every night for these last three weeks. I adore having sex with you and I want to do it all the damn time.'

Now her smile blossomed. 'Okay.'

She leaned in close and did more than let him. She met him—stroke for stroke, moan for groan. He denied the edge of desperation in his own need for physical fulfilment. He refused to face the fact that he couldn't seem to get enough of her.

All that mattered was that she was here. He'd free her of financial responsibility, he'd give her physical satisfaction, he'd offer her a lifestyle only he could provide…and she'd stay. His child would be safe. As would she.

His plan was perfectly falling into place.

CHAPTER EIGHT

SHE SHOULDN'T HAVE told him about her ex-fiancé. Leon must think she was such a naive fool. She'd done *all* the talking last night—exposed herself and all her embarrassing history. He'd shared virtually nothing, except his fantastic bedroom skills. Had he never been embarrassed? Never been rejected?

Of course not.

He couldn't reciprocate with any humanising stories of his own humiliations, because he didn't have any. And right this second she completely resented him for that. And because he was blocking her from making her own choices. Again.

'You're *not* going to work today.' He was furious.

It was almost nine the next morning. She'd slept in and he was late heading to his office because they were arguing about her plans for the day. As it was, she was feeling unsettled. She wasn't used to having a personal life, let alone everyone knowing about it. Her colleagues, her clients would all know she was sleeping with him. And the massive rocks on her finger were only going to make them even more curious. So she was tense enough without him telling her what she could and couldn't do. Again.

'Are you ashamed of what I do?' she spat sullenly.

'Do you think I'm that much of an ass?' He rolled his eyes. 'Thanks so much. You do honest work. You're good at your job. But do I want a pregnant woman carrying deliveries upstairs? No. I do not.'

'Joel would help me and it's not like I'm huge and uncomfortable already—I'm not even showing. This baby is months away, Leon. What do you want me to do all day?'

The flicker in his eyes irritated her.

'Be your concubine?' she asked tartly. '*Really?*'

'That's your fantasy, not mine.' He practically purred. 'I don't want you working as head concierge of the Cavendish any more. I want you as building manager.'

'What?' His statement undercut her argument and completely derailed her train of thought. She stared at him. 'You *what?*'

'Building manager. I want you to take over from George. It's obvious who does the work. It's Ettie. Who fixes the orders? Ettie. Who does all the rosters? Ettie. Who do the residents rely on? Ettie. You're doing it all already anyway—you might as well get paid for it.'

She simply sat there, her jaw dropped.

'I can't understand how you've not been promoted already. Actually I can: George has been claiming credit for most of your work. And then tried to blame his mistakes on you.'

Ettie did her best impersonation of a goldfish.

'I've already spoken with the management company,' he continued. 'George has agreed it's time for him to move on to a smaller establishment. And the residents committee have approved it as well.'

'Were you ever going to actually ask me if I wanted the job, or did you just expect me to jump at the chance?'

'I knew you'd jump.' He smirked. But then held up his hands. 'It's no more than deserved, Ettie.'

But she couldn't accept any promotion—not now she'd slept with the new owner.

'What's wrong now?' He released an exaggerated sigh.

'They'll think it's nepotism.'

'Why should you care what they think? The proof is in your ability to do the job. No one who knows you would ever think you *slept* your way into it.'

'Thank you *so* much.' Her blush burned.

He laughed. 'Enough. We've banished that insecurity already.'

She scowled at him. 'If it's more money, then—'

'You're already wearing my ring, Ettie. You're not backing out now. And your "more money" isn't anywhere near enough to cover Ophelia's fees for the next decade.' He brutally shut down her thinking. 'All I ask is that you take the rest of the week to recuperate from the stress of the last few days; you didn't get a lot of sleep last night. Take time to get to know this place. Then go back next week and take over fully from then.'

'You have it all mapped out,' she said stiffly.

Why did that surprise her? She swung her legs out of the bed, determined to do *something* in defiance of him.

'No. Stay there and rest.' He braced one arm either side of her and leaned over her until she fell back onto the mattress.

Quick and furious and so damned easily he proved his point, leaving her breathless and so relaxed her fight fled and all she could do was moan her approval.

'You keep distracting me with sex,' she muttered when she could breathe again.

'I'm distracting myself with sex too.' He stretched and stood, apparently energised. 'It's a good distraction.'

'But we're not solving this problem.'

'There isn't a problem,' he replied with stubborn simplicity. 'You're making a problem where there isn't one. You don't need to work today, Ettie. You've worked all your life. You've been responsible all your life. Why not take a day to have a break? You're still working—you're growing a little human.'

'I can't sit around doing nothing,' she argued. 'I've never done that.'

'So learn how to relax. Read a book. Watch TV. Sleep. Anonymously blog about your misfortunes. Whatever, just *rest*.'

She glared at him and then couldn't help laughing, as she knew he'd intended. 'Anonymously blog?'

'Yeah.' He put his hands on his hips, warming to the idea. '*My life as a billionaire's bought bride...*'

She giggled again, but then realised what she actually wanted more than anything was for him to *stay* with her today. She enjoyed his company. But he was off to maintain that millionaire income and she had to keep this as light and 'easy' as he was.

Stay in your lane, Ettie.

'I promise I'll be here for when you return, oh, lord and master,' she cooed. 'In bed,' she added on an impish urge. 'Naked.'

'Hot and wet and ready for me.' He slammed a scorching kiss onto her lips. 'Perfect.'

'I'm getting rid of all the stupid rules,' she informed him when he lifted his head. 'Starting with pets.'

'Oh, I knew that already.'

With a wriggle that was more sexual restlessness than resentment, she threw a pillow as he laughed and left the room.

No way was Ettie spending the day sitting about doing nothing. Not when her brain was fizzing with ideas for Cavendish House. She fossicked through Leon's study, marvelling at his sleek, luxurious stationery supplies. The guy had a thing for fancy fine-liner pens. Smirking, she twisted her hair into a bun and secured it in place with one and grabbed a handful of others. In the kitchen she collected some crackers, cheese and juice. She spread sheets of thick paper over the dining table to brainstorm on. It took her a while to work out the fancy 'smart house' sound system, but she got music playing eventually. Sunlight streamed through the window. She stared at the room for a moment, stunned anew. It was a gorgeous place to work. Then, energised and excited, she got down to it.

'Wow—could you make your lists any longer?'

'Oh!' Startled, Ettie glanced up to see Leon standing on the other side of the table. Her heart pounded faster at the sight of him than from the initial fright. It was impossible not to react to his presence. 'I didn't hear you come in,' she muttered, trying to regulate her breathlessness. 'What time is it?'

'After six,' he said, amusement quirking his lips.

'*No.*' She looked out of the window and saw the changing sky. 'Where'd the day go?'

'Into all those lists,' he answered drily. 'Is there any paper left?'

'Uh, some.' She glanced down. She'd smothered the table in papers, which in turn were smothered in her scribblings. 'What do you think?'

'I think you haven't rested at all today. Have you eaten?'

His concern warmed her as much as it irritated her.

'Actually I've been snacking all day and this *is* restful. I've been perched on this stool the whole time.' She saw him read through her most recent, refined list. 'You like what I've planned?'

'Yeah.' He quickly scanned her bullet points. 'You should set up a meeting with the residents' group. They'll be excited.'

'I've already emailed invitations from my phone.'

'Of course you have,' he murmured. 'That's why you got the job.'

'I can't change everything all at once,' she said earnestly. 'I know I'll need to go slow so they have time to adjust…' She trailed off as his gaze narrowed on her.

She flushed at being the focus of his intensity all over again. Every time, even though he outwardly appeared expressionless, he wasn't remote. It felt as if he was so attuned to her needs, her desires, before she was even aware of them herself. Dizzying, dazzling…*confusing.*

'Sometimes an acute, complete change is a good thing,' he said, his gaze laser-sharp on her.

'Rapid change can also be scary,' she responded pointedly. 'The staff might feel overwhelmed or defensive if they feel it's a criticism of the way things were…'

He considered it for a moment and his rare smile suddenly flashed. 'Go with your instincts; they're good.'

Excitement for her work flooded back. 'I can't wait to get started.'

'On your not-rapid changes.' He laughed and reached out, plucking the pen from her hair. '*Mine.*'

She ran her hand through her messy tangle of waves with a grimace. 'Possessive about your pens, aren't you?'

'You think I was talking about the pen?' That wicked smile flashed on his face again as he fished in his pocket for his phone. 'You okay with Italian for dinner?'

She needed a moment to catch her breath. He was just teasing, keeping it playful. Light and easy. So she'd do the same. 'Are you talking pizza or fancy?'

'How about fancy pizza?'

'Perfect.' She hopped off the stool and stretched out the cricks in her back from leaning over the table all day while he tapped a message on his phone. 'It's Friday tomorrow, then the weekend. Do you actually take weekends off or do you work through as if every day's Monday?'

'You know already.' His answering grin was rueful. 'But we could go to a recital on Saturday night if you like?' He flipped his phone around to show her the promotional information for a concert on at a nearby concert hall.

She read the headliner and stilled. It was an oboe soloist. That was *her* instrument. She looked up and saw his expectant expression. 'How did you know?'

'Saw the instrument case in your flat,' he replied. 'The music book had your name on the front. Why didn't you mention it? You've told me all about Ophelia, but you're reticent about your own dreams, Ettie.'

'*You're* calling *me* reticent?' Her jaw dropped at his temerity. 'I've told you about my ex-fiancé, my mother—'

'But not about your music. Why?'

Because it had been her secret, childish dream and she'd had to bury it. How had he picked up that it had been important—was he some kind of mind-reader? But that was impossible because she *never* thought of it now—it hurt to remember. What he'd exposed was a skeleton shipwreck of a dream that couldn't be resurrected.

'Do you wish you played now?' he asked, still intently watching her.

Her heart ached. Did he have to discover all her secrets? 'It's too late.'

'We could convert one of the lounges into a music room. You could play again.'

'No.' She chuckled softly to hide her sadness and embarrassment. Truthfully she'd been a fool to think she could've made a go of it once. 'I was never that good. I stopped when I took on a part-time job when Mum got ill. I haven't played in years. I never play now.'

'But you were good.' He looked sombre. 'That music was extremely complex.'

'You read music?'

'Sure.' He nodded.

Of course. He probably spoke more than two languages as well, only she didn't yet know it. It wasn't fair that he knew everything about her and she knew so little about him. He hadn't even left clues in his own home—nothing here told her anything more about him.

'So what instrument do you play?' she asked, determined to get an answer.

'Piano. It was compulsory to learn an instrument at school.'

'Boarding school?' She glanced at him sideways, almost afraid that if she faced him he'd fall silent again.

'Yes.'

'For your teen years?' Her curiosity burned. She wondered about everything. What were his parents really like? He had no photos of them at all here. Were they really not close? Did they really only see each other every six months or so? Had he always been this isolated?

'I went there when I was eight,' he said brusquely. 'It was good.'

She waited hopefully but he didn't add anything more.

'It's good for Ophelia too,' she said after a while. 'She gets an education and opportunities she just wouldn't otherwise.' But Ettie missed her sister hugely. If she'd won a scholarship from a day school in town, that would have been so much better. She nibbled her lower lip, thinking about her own child's future education. 'I don't want our baby going to boarding school though,' she realised with quiet conviction. It was too bad if Leon had some schooling tradition going back generations. 'I won't send him or her away. I don't care how good the school might be, there'll be schools just as good here.'

Increasing ferocity fired colour into Ettie's expression, reminding Leon of her passion and protectiveness over the dog the day they'd met. His skin seemed to tighten. He understood why she had mixed feelings about boarding school—she obviously missed her sister. But she didn't know that for him boarding school had been a blessed escape. It had been so much safer and happier than his own home.

'Okay,' he said, needing to draw a line beneath the subject. 'School here.'

He didn't want to think about the years ahead.

Right now was tough enough. She'd guessed correctly: he usually worked every day as if it were Monday. But now she was here and yeah, rapid change could be unsettling. His home was altered. Not because she'd brought in a lot of stuff, but because she'd recast the entire atmosphere—with her scent, her laughter, her smile...

Leon hadn't lived with anyone since school. He had no idea how to live with someone. No idea what he was going to do with her all weekend. He could hardly keep her tied to his bed the whole time, as appealing as that thought was. The oboe recital had been a random grasp and mainly he'd been keen to see her reaction because he was insatiably curious about her now. She fascinated him.

He gazed at the colour washing her cheeks and the sparkle shimmering in her eyes. She still glowed with the vivacity and enthusiasm that she'd worked hard all day with. Even when he'd told her not to, he'd known she would. And now that vivacity was enhanced by the filter of pure passion as she fought for something so far in the future it didn't even matter yet. She was so spirited, and so protective of their child's future.

That curling tension tightened—constricting his throat, his chest. He couldn't resist the need to get nearer to her. He wanted her heat, her willingness, her total surrender to his touch. There was something deeper too, something so powerful that he couldn't examine it too closely.

Just want.

He reassured himself. But it was strong.

The weekend plans were irrelevant. Suddenly he had no spare thought for the past, or the future. His immediate need was too intense.

He pulled her against him. He didn't know how else to release the heavy pressure crushing his chest, threatening to cleave him open. He didn't want to be torn apart and have any of this emotion *exposed*. Not memories. Not pain. He wanted nothing but pleasure with her. *Now.*

He slid his hand into her glossy hair and tilted her head back to expose her pretty neck. Her soft lips parted and emotion glittered in her eyes. Emotion he refused to analyse. He didn't know how. He certainly didn't stop to examine his own. He was only seeking her consent—to lose them both in that fiery desire. And he got it—there in her crystal, cloudless eyes.

She might appear vulnerable, but she was strong. He could see her energy pulsing in that soft space at the base of her neck. He bent his head and kissed her hard and deep, releasing all the passion and lust into her, until that weight blocking his chest eased and heat swirled in its place. She was so intoxicating, he sank to his knees, determined to gift her every ounce of pleasure he could. Nothing else mattered. Nothing but now. Here. Her pleasure. Her sighs.

He cupped her full breasts, knowing they were tender and more sensitive, teasing until he felt her need deepening, until he heard her breathy little pleas. Then it was that sweet, wet, secret part of her that he couldn't resist baring, touching, *tasting*.

'Lean on me,' he muttered as he felt her trembling response.

She was hot and lush and he craved every inch, every lick of her. She pressed her hands on his shoulders for balance, her legs spread as wide as they could against the constraints of the panties he'd pulled halfway down her thighs. He revelled in her quivering, in her desperate cries. His blood flowed freely now—warming him, releasing him from that tight, painful pressure. This was what he wanted. He pressed closer still and destroyed her.

Ettie woke late and saw the fresh juice, plain crackers and sliced fruit on a tray beside the bed. She smiled ruefully. Leon was unfailingly attentive and good at anticipating almost every one of her needs. She could hardly bear to think of those insane moments last night when he'd knelt at her feet and made her mad with desire. In that dangerously seductive stance, she'd felt like his queen, as if he couldn't exist in that moment without touching her. He'd made her feel *wanted* in a way she'd never felt wanted before. And he'd made her feel such thrilling, intense pleasure, such total exhilaration, that she'd screamed until she was hoarse.

In the aftermath she'd been so dazed she could barely stand. Her wits had been too scrambled for her to be able to lighten it at all, to even think of *reciprocating*. He'd straightened her clothing and told her to go and tidy herself quick-smart, because their restaurant booking was soon.

Once more, it wasn't just any restaurant and it

wasn't pizza. It was award-winning, exclusive and so expensive they didn't bother putting the prices on the menu. There was no choice as to what they got to eat either. That was because the food the world-renowned chef prepared was so exquisite, no one sane would ever think to complain or argue with the selection. Pure perfection. And absolute decadence.

She'd been so tired she'd fallen asleep on the drive home. She'd woken as he'd carried her up to his bed. And once there, she'd realised she wasn't *quite* as sleepy as all that. He'd laughed, indulging her again in that searing, soul-destroying sex. Again. And then again.

Just sex, Ettie. Good sex. Stupendous. But just sex.

But thank goodness he seemed to be as hungry for it as she.

Now he'd gone to work and she had another day to herself before the weekend. Another day to come to terms with the fragile future they were building.

But there was imbalance between them and it wasn't their bank balances. He knew *everything*. Her stupid mistakes of the past. Even her sorry childhood dream of becoming a musician. Every little secret. Furthermore, he'd done so much for her—the ring, the home, the job…and things so much more intimate than that. He turned her inside out, made her mindless with pleasure. He'd given her pretty much everything.

But what had she given *him*? What had he *let* her give him—other than her body? He didn't open up, didn't let her in. She breathed out and reminded herself it was very early days. He didn't trust her yet and he had a thing about people always wanting things from him—he'd joked about it but there'd been a tiny truth there.

What if she was to give *him* something?

Problem was, it wasn't as if he needed her to *buy* him anything and it wasn't as if she had vast amounts of money to splash out either. And it wasn't about a *thing*, it was about doing something thoughtful, to show that she was invested in making this work the same way he was. That she could be attentive too. But she knew so little, she couldn't think of what to do or get, and she was good at getting things for privileged people.

With a sigh, she got out of bed and returned the plate and glass to the gleaming kitchen. She caught sight of the shiny new dog bowls sitting uselessly on the counter. She paused, her gaze fixed on them. Leon said he'd never had a puppy, but he'd been surprisingly willing to take Toby. She'd had a feeling that he'd been more keen on that than he'd expressed. It hadn't all been about getting her up to that penthouse in Cavendish House. She remembered how he'd gently patted the dog.

Her heart pounded as she turned over the wisp of an idea in her mind. It would be a huge risk. But instinct told her it would be worth it. It would be right.

Go with your instincts; they're good.

She turned her back on the lists she'd left on the table and ran back upstairs to get dressed.

Ettie Roberts had a mission.

CHAPTER NINE

LEON TRIED TO stay at work. Tried to concentrate. Tried not to think about the weekend ahead. It wasn't that he didn't want her there, he did, but it felt as if the ground was shifting and he couldn't quite hold his balance. In the end he gave up resisting and let the weight coiling within push him home.

'Ettie?' He rolled his shoulders, trying to ease that tension as he shucked off his jacket and shoes.

'Leon?' Her answering call was pitched high.

'Who else?' he asked drily, following the direction of her voice to the kitchen.

He fought to restrain the urge to go straight up and kiss her until the tightness in his chest eased again. Not two nights running—he had more control than that, right? But in the doorway he paused to draw breath. She looked amazing to his hungry eyes— jeans, T-shirt, hair twisted out of the way and secured with a pen again. His again.

'I wasn't sure what time you'd be home... You're early.' Her face was flushed but it wasn't that usual blush of sensuality.

And she couldn't quite maintain eye contact, which initially intrigued, then concerned him. He strolled closer, trying to take it easy, but his instincts were firing. Something was off. 'What've you been up to today?' he asked. 'No more lists?'

The table was scrupulously tidy.

His pulse began to pound. Why couldn't she look at him? Why was she so flushed? Why so silent?

At that exact moment, he heard a strange scratching coming from behind him. Ettie froze, her eyes wide. He cocked his head and narrowed his gaze on her. 'What's that?'

'Hmm?' she mumbled.

'Ettie?'

The noise sounded again and there was no hiding the guilty look in her eyes—her face was far too expressive.

Now she pressed her lips together in an oddly nervous manner. 'I've done something,' she blurted. 'I got you a present.'

He stilled. 'You what?'

'I got you a present. I hope you don't mind.'

Why would he mind? He actually couldn't remember the last time anyone had got him a present. He didn't have a bunch of friends he did birthday celebrations with and his parents definitely didn't send him anything. Not at Christmas either.

There was another scratching sound. And then a high-pitched yelp. Not Ettie. Not *human*.

Leon spun around. 'Ettie?'

She scuttled past him and he watched her hunch

down by a box he'd not noticed before because he'd only had eyes for her. Leon couldn't move. It was a big box.

Then Ettie stood and walked towards him and she was holding—

'He was the runt,' she said all in a rush. 'I don't know quite what breed he is…a mix of many, and I know he's not handsome like Toby, but he wasn't going to have a chance otherwise.'

Leon stared at the creature in Ettie's arms. 'You got me a puppy?'

His heart beat too fast; his lungs felt as if they were in a swiftly tightening vice.

'You have space here.' She sounded as breathless as he felt. 'You could train him to go to the office with you, or he can stay here and play in the garden, or he could come to the Cavendish with me…we can make it work. I just thought you'd like him.' She stepped closer and literally shoved the puppy into his arms.

Leon instinctively grabbed the animal but inside he'd frozen.

'You said you'd not had a dog, but I thought you'd quite wanted Toby. I thought…' She trailed off as she finally looked up at him. 'I don't really know what I thought.' She stared into his eyes, her own growing more concerned by the second. 'Do you mind?' It was a whisper.

Leon couldn't move. He couldn't actually breathe. That pressure crushing his chest was too heavy on his lungs.

'He's about four months old, they think,' she said.

'All vaccinated. If they couldn't rehome him they were going to—'

'He's a rescue puppy?' he croaked, determinedly pushing past the immobility to glance down at the puppy who'd settled so quickly in his arms. Small, with bottomless brown eyes that had a heart-wrenching hint of sadness, mostly black hair but with patches of silvery white…he was ridiculously cute.

'Yes.'

Leon cleared his throat. 'Does he have a name?'

She shook her head. 'You'll have to give him one.'

He didn't want to do that. He couldn't.

Memory washed over him. He'd held a tiny puppy like this only once before years ago. It had been small and fragile like this one. It had been his…but only for a little while.

He stilled as past and present blurred and the reality of their future hit hard. He didn't know if he could do this. *Any* of this.

'Leon? Don't you like him?'

He huffed out a hard-caught breath. Of course he liked him. How could he not?

'What is it?' she asked softly. 'Leon?' Her eyes suddenly filled. 'Did I do the wrong thing?'

'No,' he muttered quickly. She was so sweet, she didn't realise. 'No.'

'Then what is it?' She wasn't just sweet, she was astute. She saw right through him.

And he couldn't bear that. 'It's not important,' he snapped, needing to shut her down.

'If it's not important, it won't matter if you tell me, will it?'

He almost smiled at her simple logic, but he was stuck, unable to escape the most painful of memories. 'You don't want my poor-little-rich-boy sob story.'

'Yes—'

'It is what it is,' he interrupted awkwardly. 'I can't change it.'

He didn't want questions, didn't want to remember. His mouth was dry and he felt too big to be holding something so small. He didn't want to hold it close. He didn't want to feel. He needed time to think. But Ettie kept looking at him with those beseeching sea-green eyes and when she did that he couldn't seem to think at all.

'Leon—'

'My neighbour gave me a puppy,' he growled before she could say anything else in that husky, sweet voice. She was so frustratingly curious. 'But my mother got rid of it after a few weeks.'

'Got rid of it?' Ettie frowned. 'You don't mean—'

'Yeah, I do mean.' The words just fell out. A bald, uncontrollable burn of memory. The disappearance. The shocking silence and the absolute emptiness inside him. 'They weren't interested in me—I was their tick-the-box baby. They were busy with their careers. Their affairs. They just wanted a trophy and heir. They didn't want the actual *child*. The actual child was…' He broke off, tearing his gaze from Ettie to focus on the small dog that had nestled so easily into his arms. It was so trusting. But he hadn't been able to protect that first puppy...

He dragged in a harsh breath. He shouldn't have said anything, but now he'd started, ripping open that old wound so it oozed poison and pus. He couldn't stop the truth of it spewing out.

'One child was more than enough for my mother to handle and, as I was a child of privilege, it was her duty to educate me on my duty and ensure I wasn't spoiled.'

'Not spoiled?' Ettie echoed softly.

He looked back into her expressive face and watched as understanding dawned.

'She was cruel?' she said.

Leon couldn't bear the sympathy in her eyes. Why had he said anything? He hated remembering how weak he'd once been. He never wanted anyone to have power over him again. Not physical. Not emotional. Not contractual. Never again would he be that vulnerable. That powerless.

'Leon...'

'I was extremely fortunate.' He tried to plug the information leak, tried to squash all that horror back in the depths of his ribcage. 'I had the best education.'

Never show weakness. Never admit to failure. Always fight.

'But she hurt you. Not just your puppy. She hurt *you.*'

So many times, in so many small ways. He froze but was still unable to think, unable to hold back that pressure bursting within him.

Ettie stepped closer. 'She hit you?'

'Too obvious.' The words escaped, heedless of his battle to keep silent. 'She'd force me to shower in freezing water. Five minutes. Reciting equations, verbs, some poem. Whatever lesson I needed to be drilled in. I had to say it aloud over and over again. That was one of the many...' He paused, drawing in a hard breath. 'Just little things she did to...'

'Torture you.'

'Toughen me up.' He grimaced. 'Cold showers, barefoot runs in the frost, two hours locked in a dark cupboard if I answered back or worse...all things that left no physical mark, but would teach me to control myself. Not cry. Not show weakness.'

Not anger. Not love either. Not any emotions. He'd learned calm instead—to close down, stay still, breathe, *think*. Except he couldn't do any of that now with the way Ettie was looking at him.

'It worked,' he said, stubbornly rejecting what he saw in her eyes. 'I grew resilience. Definitely gained independence. Didn't rely on anyone else for anything.'

'You couldn't tell your father?'

The last sliver of Leon's heart shrivelled. 'He knew.' And he'd done nothing.

'You couldn't tell anyone else?'

There hadn't been anyone else. There'd never been any physical marks left on him. But he had the feeling his old neighbour at their summer house suspected. That was why she'd given him that puppy. Calix had been the runt of the litter, just like this little guy.

His mother had relented too easily—said yes to that nice old neighbour. She'd said yes so swiftly, bubbling with faux gratitude. He should've known it was too good to last. He was to perform. He was to lead. He was to remain in charge of everything. The loss she then subjected him to was to build his fight—the puppy was a mere tool for him to learn pain and to protect himself from feeling it again. Never to lose again.

It hurts when important things are taken from you. The dog isn't important. Our company is.

He'd never trusted again either.

'That's why you were happy to go away to school,' Ettie whispered.

'It was a relief.' Leon wanted nothing more than to freeze back up inside. 'But she'd hit me in other ways. When you're told something over and over and over, you begin to believe it, especially when the person telling you is supposed to be your protector.' She'd shut him off from everyone. Her words echoed in his head.

'*They only want to be friends because of your money. They want to use you. But you haven't done anything to deserve what you have. You don't deserve it.*'

He realised far too late that he'd said it all aloud. Ettie's expression was appalled. He turned away, unable to look at her any more. If he didn't look at her he might get himself back under control.

'My mother was determined to make me strong enough, good enough to take over the specific challenges of a multimillion-dollar empire. To become the tough, decisive boss I'd need to be. I tried hard to please her.' To please both his parents. He'd tried for so long. 'Eventually I realised I was never going to. Nothing would make her happy. So I decided that I'd never be the heir they'd worked so *diligently* to raise. Not by going off the rails—that would have pleased her, I think. It would have proven that I was as "weak" as she'd said I was. So no drugs, no booze-fuelled parties, no threesomes…' He almost smiled. 'I turned my back on that "duty" and rejected the inheritance they offered. I'll never work for the company, or take charge of it. Instead I worked alone and earned more, just to spite her. I worked every holiday and left home the second I was old enough.'

'To make your own way.'

He'd pushed to the top relentlessly—taken huge risks, worked insane hours. Because he didn't want a cent of his parents' money. Didn't want the 'glory' of running their empire. After all, he'd not *deserved* it—so he'd built his own.

He didn't need them. He didn't need *anyone*.

Now he carried the sleeping puppy back to the box and saw the small bed Ettie had got for it inside. He carefully put the puppy in. Why had he said anything? He never talked to anyone about this. Bracing himself against the silence, he turned back and saw her face. His body tightened.

'I don't want your pity.' All that emotion emptied again. He couldn't stand to see the sympathy in her eyes. 'I cannot be pitied. Look at everything I have, everything I've done.'

'Yeah, you're amazing,' she whispered. 'But you don't let people in.'

'Why would I want to?' He turned to look back at the sleeping dog.

Yet he knew he had to—his own child was the game changer. And it was happening *too soon*. He'd never wanted one, but now one was on the way and he wanted it to have everything he hadn't and still didn't have. Self-sufficiency was key to his own existence, yet he was human enough not to want that for his own child. Thank goodness the baby had Ettie.

He tried to be calm, to breathe, to think. But his heart thundered and his lungs hurt. His whole chest was still bound in tension.

Leon stood so still, Ettie almost believed he wasn't breathing. But as she neared, she could feel the vibrations rolling off him. She sensed the power he was exerting to hold back and press everything back down deep. He'd been appallingly hurt and she'd had absolutely no idea. He'd hidden it so well, for so long.

She might not have had a father, but she'd had a mother who'd loved her, who'd at least wanted the best for her. And she'd had her sister.

Leon had been utterly isolated. The witch hadn't even let him keep his dog. His father hadn't stood up for him. The horror of it broke her heart. That he'd been treated as a project, not a person.

While she'd grown up with nothing but love, he'd

grown up with everything but. No wonder he was remote and controlled and untrusting. And right now she knew he regretted saying anything at all. While there mightn't have been physical marks, there were definitely emotional scars. Five minutes beneath a frigid torrent of water must've felt like an eternity. Two hours in a dark cupboard for a small boy must've been pure hell.

'Leon—'

'Don't.'

She knew he was withdrawing. Rebuilding his walls to shut her out again. She couldn't let that happen. Not yet.

'Don't think that this is going to change everything just because you've told me a few things,' she said, trying to reach him. 'We're just getting to know each other, that's all. That helps build trust.'

'Don't actions speak louder than words, Ettie?' The strain was evident in his hoarseness. 'Can't you trust me already? I'm not your dad or your ex. I haven't left you.'

Not physically. But emotionally he was walking out of that door. And he was turning the focus from himself to her, to help his escape.

'Leon—'

'Have I betrayed you?' he flared.

'No.' She welcomed the resurgence of his emotion and stepped closer. 'But there's action and there's *action*.'

His default response was to close down all intimacy other than the physical. It was the only way she could think to keep him here *with* her.

'Look,' he cleared his throat, 'you're going to make a wonderful mother, Ettie. I know you'll care for this child in a way I was never cared for. But I can only do what I do.' He frowned as if he was struggling to think. 'I'm good at taking control in a crisis.'

Yes. Because his whole life had been a crisis. He'd been locked for ever in a fight for survival, to win, to be free. When had he last taken the time to just breathe? When had he ever let someone else make the calls and shoulder even a little bit of his burden?

'You have to take control because you've never had anyone you could count on.' She placed her hand on his chest.

He didn't reply. The agony churning in his eyes, the blistering beat of his heart beneath her fingers, said it all. He didn't trust anyone. She didn't blame him; she had trust issues of her own. But maybe in time he could learn to trust *her*? Maybe—eventually—they could be a true team?

'Can't you relinquish control to me?' she asked softly, spreading her hand wider and slowly sliding it down his chest. 'Just once?' She felt his muscles tighten beneath her touch, saw awareness flare in his eyes.

'Are you still feeling insecure about your sexual experience?' he asked gruffly.

No. This wasn't about *her*. But this was the language she knew he understood and it could be their starting point, right?

'Don't you know what you do to me?' he asked harshly as she slid her hand to his belt and twisted her fingers to release the buckle.

She shook her head. That was what she wanted most of all—to see him. To know him. 'Let me see.' She lifted her chin and dared him, unfastening the buttons of his shirt without hesitation. 'Let me do it.'

He didn't stop her. But he didn't help. Like a statue ablaze—the tension thrummed from him as she pushed back the two halves of his shirt so she could see—touch—his burning skin.

'Just let me,' she whispered.

She reached up on tiptoe and kissed along his jaw, aching for the years of sufferance and isolation he'd endured. He didn't lower his chin to meet her lips with his.

'I don't want your sympathy,' he growled, rigid and angry.

'Just as I don't want your money,' she answered.

He pulled back his head to look down at her then. 'This isn't about money.'

'It isn't about sympathy either. This is about *caring*, Leon.' She cupped his jaw with one hand, and slid her other over his chest, tracing the strength and heat. Skin on skin. 'This is about you opening up and letting me in. Let me in.'

'You don't need to take care of me.'

'But you get to take care of me? Next you'll try telling me not to breathe,' she muttered back at him. 'Screw your control, Leon.'

With a sudden forceful push, she pressed him

against the wall. His eyes widened and his hands automatically spanned her waist.

'I'm taking control.' She kissed her way down his chest. Her own passion was unleashed. She wanted to *truly* touch him. She wanted to show him—

'You think?' He hauled her back up to kiss her hard and deep, his anger igniting.

'I *know*,' she said when she tore her lips free.

A crazy kind of confidence she'd never before felt fired through her veins. She knew what to do. What she wanted. She showered his body with kisses, with light, teasing touches of her fingertips, with swirls of her tongue, before letting her lips slide closer.

Her own heat increased the more she heard his uneven breathing, the more she felt his tension build. She stepped back for a moment to slide her own clothes off. Slowing when she saw the way he was leaning back against the wall, his feet planted wide apart, watching her strip. She was no real beauty, definitely no model-type, but clearly it didn't matter.

Only when she was fully naked did she step forward again. She unzipped his trousers, pulled them and his boxers down. She knelt in front of him as he'd knelt before her only last night.

She heard his growl—of warning, of *want*. She smiled and kissed closer, closer, but she didn't take him in her mouth. Not yet. It was enough to let him enjoy looking. She saw his hands curl into fists, his knuckles whitening. He liked what she was doing. But he was still holding back. She didn't want him to hold back.

She licked up the length of him and then looked up. 'Lie down.'

He shot her a look but complied with her request.

Ettie simply stared for a moment at the sheer magnificence of him outstretched on the floor before her. He still said nothing but his raging erection and ragged breathing were all the encouragement she needed. Her mouth watered and that confidence flooded her again.

She straddled him and ran her hands over his body. He was so still. Letting her. Yet resisting her inwardly. He'd learned such control. He needed to unlearn it.

And she just needed to touch him. She was firm. Gentle. Reverent. Then rougher. As she released her grip on her own desire, her pace picked up, her intentions deepened, her need coiled. Her breathing shallowed, her heat spiked.

He was so strong. So alone. So worthy of so much more. And now she was angry. He should have had everything. She would give him everything *she* could right now. With a blind kind of fury, she ached to make him feel the way he made her feel—*wanted*. So. Damn. Much.

She slid up the length of his body, desperately kissing him, stroking, sucking him hard and then grinding her heat on him, until he flipped—literally holding her to him and flipping them both so he was above her...within her.

'*Yes*,' she cried out as he thrust to the hilt.

But he stopped—straining—his eyes closed, his jaw clenched as he fought to regain his control.

'Don't stop,' she ordered, gazing up at him. 'Don't shut me out.'

His hands gripped her thighs deliciously hard. She knew he couldn't resist this for much longer. He shuddered as she moved beneath him sinuously, easing her own ache, enticing him to complete abandonment.

His eyes opened. 'I don't like losing control of my emotions, Ettie,' he grated.

'Is it losing control of them?' she challenged him. 'Or is it just expressing them?'

He was still for a searing moment more. Then she saw the flare and felt his sudden shift. He snatched the pen securing her hair—freeing it into a wild tumble around her shoulders. He wound thick hanks of it around his wrists—literally binding her to him and cradling her head in his fingers so he could see into her eyes, so he could devour her mouth. The tug was strong, but not painful as her head tilted back at his pull—exposing her mouth, her neck, her breasts to his ravenous, rough kisses.

'I like it,' she admitted with low, savage hunger. 'I like touching you. I like seeing you like this. I want you like this.'

'On the edge?' he growled, twisting his hands again to shorten the tie between them.

'Over it,' she said brazenly. 'With me.'

He swore bluntly and drove into her, again and again. Ruthlessly, out of control, he claimed his place in her very core—pushing harder, faster, deeper. This wasn't fun or easy or light. It was the most bared, the most touched she'd ever been. The lump in her throat ached. She'd been alone too. She'd been alone so long, but right now—he was here, right here, literally bound to her. Inside her *totally*. Her eyes stung because she was exposed—vulnerable and shaking and so damn needy of *this*. His kiss, his possession. She felt the wild emotion storming through him and into her, only to transform again into something wonderful that they then rode together. He growled again as she arched, pressing herself closer still, wrapping her legs and arms tightly around him, holding him so they were utterly inseparable. His kiss devastated her. Unleashed emotion rippled between them like electricity—a power surge energising them both into frantic, clawing creatures seeking oblivion in this dark, magic world they made together. She gasped as he thrust harder and harder. He was so powerful. And she so complete. All thought was gone, all words. There was only animal sensation, animal sounds... and then screaming, orgasmic agony.

Leon flinched, suddenly wide awake. It was completely dark. Despite the warmth of the soft woman curled next to him, he was freezing. His heart was pounding as if he'd been sprinting for his life. He'd woken like this so many times in his youth and he hated it.

Despite the pleasure he'd had with Ettie tonight, he was now tossed back into that old torment. That stupid talk had stirred up thoughts. Memories. Feelings. *Fear*.

He should have kept it in, resisted his own damn

temptation. But that gift, Ettie's sweetness, cracked him open. Now he tried to empty his mind again but those malevolent memories swirled, relentless. They'd been woken.

He'd kept it all buried for so long—had hidden that dark, incomplete side of himself from everyone. Living alone it didn't matter, it was easy. But in marriage?

He didn't want to poison her with it. He wished he'd never told her. To complain of a little punishment? Of loneliness? He'd been as weak as his mother had warned. What he needed was his control back.

He slid out of bed silently so he didn't wake Ettie and quickly checked the small puppy. It was fast asleep and warm in its little bed. Leon opened up his laptop in the lounge and tried to work. But his mind was fragmented and he'd achieved little by the time dawn finally began to lighten the dark.

He showered, standing for a long time under the steaming jet—trying to relax. He'd get through the weekend, he'd fall back into bed with her...

But he hadn't even made it to Saturday before falling apart. Having her this close was confusing, constricting...those stirred-up memories still prickled like thorns in a blood-splattered bouquet in a damn low-budget horror film. Reaching out, he flicked the faucet to cold and suffered the pelting icy droplets. They were like little knives, pinkening up soft skin. Those memories surged.

He braced. He'd beaten them a long time ago. Banished them. And he'd banish them again now because he was not that boy any more. He had control. He flicked the faucet back to warm. Yeah. He had *power*. And he would make this work.

He'd talked about it with Ettie—told her far more than he'd ever intended. Surely he'd satisfied her infernal curiosity at last? So now it was done and behind them for ever.

He'd get this back to the practical, responsible arrangement he needed it to be.

He breathed in and quietly walked to the bedroom to grab some clothes. Then he got back to his computer. Focused. Calm. Ready.

But Ettie walked into the lounge an hour later, looking like sunshine in a simple denim skirt and white T-shirt. One look and he felt that hard-wrestled-for control slip again. Every time he so much as looked at her it was like that thing bound tightly within him was loosened. But it was something he didn't want released. Not ever.

'You're working already?' she asked.

He nodded, fighting the urge to reach out and touch her. To use sex as his distraction again, as she'd teased the other day...

But last night—how good she'd felt, how intense that had been with her...that hadn't just been distraction. It had been much more than simple, mindless fun. And it couldn't be like that again.

'I've fed the puppy; he's asleep again,' he said after clearing his throat. 'We'll take him for a walk later.'

She nodded and sauntered through to the kitchen looking like the sexiest, sweetest thing he'd ever seen.

He breathed out as she left. See? He could resist. She'd claimed control, but he had it back. Just.

Oh, who was he kidding?

Only now he realised the troubling truth: *she* was his weakness—Ettie Roberts herself. His slide into addiction had already started and he hadn't realised because she felt so good. But *she* was what he craved—*all* the time. But he couldn't use her in that way, as if she were his personal opiate. He had to dial it back. He *had* lost control last night and he'd not expressed anything other than pure, selfish greed.

He refused to be all over her. Sure, they'd sleep together and they'd have this baby, but he'd pull himself together properly and remind them *both* that this was just another business arrangement. That was all it could ever be.

CHAPTER TEN

ETTIE WAS ACUTELY relieved when Monday finally arrived. It wasn't that the weekend had been awful... She and Leon had walked the puppy, wandered around the markets, watched a movie rather than go to that concert—her pick. He'd driven her out of town specially to dine at another amazing restaurant... It was as if he was determined they'd be a normal couple—albeit one with luxurious experiences. She knew he wanted to make this work and she knew he'd be loyal. He had his own brand of duty and honour burned in him. He had everything else too—humour, looks, a bank balance big enough to make anyone's eyes water. And he was so attentive, always ensuring she had what she needed.

Almost all she needed.

But there'd been no more mad, unrestrained sex on the floor, in the kitchen, in the lounge...in fact there'd been no touching at all until darkness fell. But then when it did...?

They'd come together with a wordless intensity that neither of them had addressed afterwards. Neither Saturday nor Sunday. But all through both nights that raw, unrestrained passion had been unleashed. That genie was well out of the bottle now. Leon had made her moan and shake, he'd stripped her back to pure nerves and he'd roared with her, riding her hard. Again. Again. Again. Through the darkness they'd clung to each other, almost crazed with need. Neither of them could get enough and neither of them denied it. Until daylight. Then they were returned to that beautifully curated lifestyle of breakfast at a cute deli, a walk in the park, pondering his next art selection at an elite auction house...but no argument or discussion of anything *deep*. And that was why she was relieved by the prospect of work. She needed the time away from him so she could *think*. Because it wasn't quite right—not since that acutely profound moment on Friday night.

Now she shimmied into her uniform and brushed her hair into submission, ready to face her first day in her new position.

'Here...' Leon was in the kitchen, dressed in a charcoal suit, looking more remote and businesslike than ever. 'Something for your first day as manager.'

She picked up the beautiful business satchel he'd pushed across the counter towards her. She saw the gold insignia and drew in a steadying breath. This wasn't some knock-off from the street markets, this was real leather, from a real luxury label. 'You didn't have to—'

'Look inside.' He sipped his coffee and watched her. She suddenly felt nervous, because his gaze seemed especially dark this morning—the amber glow was absent. She reached for the slim box tucked inside. Pressing her lips together, she lifted the lid.

It was a pen, but not just any pen. The distinctive white star on the cap told her that, as did the intricately engraved gold nib. 'Leon—'

'Now you don't need to steal mine.' His gaze drifted to her hair and seemed to darken some more. 'You can keep your hair up with it.'

She shook her head. 'I'd be too afraid I'd lose it.' She knew it was worth a crazy amount of money. And it was beautiful—feminine and perfect. But she didn't know if she could keep accepting these kinds of gifts.

'Well,' he set the coffee cup down with a slight bang, 'you can use it to sign the contract in the folder.'

'Contract?'

'The sooner it's signed off, the sooner I can organise the accounts.'

Accounts? With a growing sense of foreboding Ettie looked into the soft leather case again and drew out the slim Manila folder. She opened it and saw several pages of neat type. She stilled as she read the title—it was the prenuptial contract between her and Leon. Their *arrangement* in all its ugly glory.

'I'll need to take time to read it properly,' she muttered, feeling a hit of dizziness as she saw the lists of numbers—*remuneration*. She'd forgotten about their 'deal' over the weekend. She'd been too busy trying to breach his defences again the way she had on Friday night. Too busy trying to restore her own inner equilibrium. And she'd failed on both counts.

His lips twisted. 'Sure. Get it back to me later today.'

She frowned as she studied one page more carefully—the itemised list of her *benefits*. 'This monthly allowance…is for groceries and everything?'

'No, it's your personal allowance.'

But it was more than what she was paid for her job at Cavendish House! She looked up to glare at him.

'You need new clothes and things…'

Her fury mounted and he fell silent at the expression in her eyes. Yeah, he knew she was insulted. But what was worse was that she knew he'd done this deliberately to engender such a reaction in her. Well, it had worked.

'And I get an annual bonus each year for remaining married to you?' she clarified with barely disguised rage.

He lifted that damned coffee cup to his lips again.

'You think I'll respond to that kind of financial incentive?'

'Doesn't everyone?' he asked coolly.

After she'd opened up to him so completely? After what they'd shared on Friday night? Hurt swept over her in a violent wave. Yet immediately after it followed a deep resignation—and *regret*. Because she remembered she'd *already* responded to a financial inducement. It was why she'd agreed to marry him in the first place. This was just the painful reminder of that reality—in cold black and white print.

She shuffled the odious pages together and shoved them into the damned gorgeous bag, tossing the pen in too, not bothering with the perfect little presentation box. 'I'd better get to work; I don't want to be late.'

'I'll drop you.'

'No need.' She turned a huge smile on him as she marched out of the room. 'I'm happy to walk.'

To her enormous relief—and no small amount of regret—he didn't follow her. She breathed quick, steadying breaths all the way to Cavendish House but her nausea had returned. And all her horror.

Yet why should she be so angry about it? Shouldn't she take this as the business opportunity it was? He was giving her everything she could ever want, right?

Because he didn't really want this. Not with her.

He'd lifted that curtain and told her about his life and he regretted it. Not just a wince of embarrassment, but an excoriating extent of regret. He'd pretended he didn't, he didn't show any outward emotion, but she'd seen it eating him, she'd sensed his withdrawal as he sought to rebuild walls he thought were weakened. All weekend she'd hoped—but he hadn't opened up again. Instead he'd made it all about *her.* As if he was determined to make her *happy*—as if it was another job for him to entertain her. Despite their intimacy, the distance she'd felt between them wasn't breached. And she knew the effort he'd made was unsustainable. If it was this hard for him now, she couldn't see how it was going to work for long in the future.

And he'd been busy in the background, hadn't he? Working out his damned clinical contract to seal them both into nothing but a seedy money-for-marriage transaction.

To think she'd actually thought for a moment that they might've become something *more*. To think she'd actually had that fantasy of happy-ever-after. That she'd actually had hope that with time…

One look at that contract and she knew there was no chance. His regret was all-consuming. She'd feel sorry for him if she wasn't so hurt. Did he really think so little of her? Think she'd accept money to make their marriage last month by month?

Now she'd never felt as exposed or as insecure in all her life. Not when her mother had got her diagnosis, or when her ex had texted to tell her the wedding was off. Neither compared to the uncertainty she felt now. Her heart raced as if she'd sprinted her way to work. And now she had to maintain the lie in front of her friends—act ecstatic and in love and all that…it was too hard and all she wanted to do was cry.

Work. Be like Leon. Get it done.

She *had* to get it done. She couldn't let that contract ruin her career as well. She'd worked too hard for it. She just needed to find the time to work out what she was going to do about Leon next. She'd have to do that later.

So she smiled with pure determination as Joel held the door to the concierge office open for her when she arrived, and when he bowed as she walked through.

'Stop it.' She tried to laugh it off.

'You're the boss now… I have to bow and scrape.'

'Ettie,' Jess squealed and leapt up from the seat

she'd been sitting on, obviously waiting for her arrival. 'You should *hear* the rumours about you.' She pounced on her and grabbed Ettie's hand, her eyes bugging as she inspected the emerald and diamonds. 'OMG, it's true. I'm *so* thrilled for you.' Jess swept her up in a giant hug. 'When you fainted and he carried you up to the penthouse, it was the most *romantic* thing I've ever seen.'

Ettie hid her face in Jess's shoulder. Her friend's congratulations were heartfelt but she felt hideously awkward. Her engagement wasn't romantic at all, but a business arrangement with benefits.

'And you've worked so hard, you deserve your promotion,' Joel said a little gruffly.

'He's pleased because he gets promoted too,' Jess teased Joel with sparkling eyes. 'What you deserve, Ettie, is *happiness*.'

Ettie blinked back the shockingly sudden surge of tears. She'd worked alongside these guys for years and seeing them this happy for her was…overwhelming. And awkward. So awkward. She blew out a quick breath and smiled as Joel and Jess left the office to get on with their jobs. She could hold it together. It was just hormones and tiredness and the horror of that awful agreement that she couldn't think about right now…

The morning went swiftly because it was perfectly, blessedly busy. But just as she'd finally settled into the swing of it, someone called her to the front desk.

'Hey!'

Ettie's legs suddenly weakened. 'Ophelia?'

'Yes!' Her little sister rushed over and pulled her into a huge hug, managing to dance a small jig at the same time.

'Why are you here? Is everything okay?' Ettie's heart thudded.

'Everything is fabulous.'

Ophelia leaned back and Ettie got a good look at her. Her sister, taller than Ettie, was stunning even in her slightly faded second-hand blazer. Her hair was chestnut and shining and her skin and smile just glowed with health.

'I'm in London for a debating tournament.'

'Of course you are.' Ettie laughed at her gorgeous, geeky sister. 'Why didn't you tell me you were coming?'

'I wasn't sure I could get here. I only have an hour and then I have to get back for the next round.'

'You sneaked out?'

'Well, *duh*.' Ophelia laughed. 'Because I'm so excited for you. I couldn't come to London and not *see* you.'

'Come into the office.' Ettie bit her lip and led her sister into a private space.

She'd phoned Ophelia at Friday lunchtime, after her trip to the dog shelter. She'd told her about moving in with Leon and the baby and *almost* everything.

But not quite all. She could never tell her sister the deal she'd struck with Leon. She could never explain the intricacies of that.

'Is he here?' Ophelia asked as soon as the door

was closed, her eyes shining so brightly that Ettie couldn't hold her gaze.

'No, he's in his office. He has meetings.' Right now Ettie was so glad he'd moved out of Cavendish House.

'When can I meet him?' Ophelia bounced on her toes. 'I can't wait to meet him.'

Churning hot acid burned up Ettie's throat. This was so much worse than the lie to Jess and Joel. 'He's a busy guy.'

'You have to come up and see me and bring him. Please! You have to come soon.'

Ettie nodded. But she didn't want Ophelia to meet him. She didn't want this to become that real.

'What's wrong?' Ophelia paused, a slight frown forming on her face.

'Nothing, I'm just…surprised to see you.' Ettie summoned a bright smile, but she and Ophelia were close. Too close—because right now Ophelia saw right through her. She had to act as if it were perfect. It was perfect, wasn't it?

'Good surprised or bad surprised?'

'Good—but if you get into trouble for sneaking out from debating, I won't be happy.'

Ophelia smiled but her gaze was still too watchful. 'Do you love him, Ettie?'

Ettie's throat constricted. She couldn't answer that question. She couldn't answer that one even to herself. But her face burned with a blush.

'Are you happy?' Ophelia's smile was so sweet, so caring, so concerned.

This was the moment to lie. The moment she *had* to lie. But she still couldn't get her voice to work. She made herself nod even as a tear spilled over.

'*Ettie*.' Ophelia wrapped her arms around her. 'I'm worried.'

'Hormones,' she croaked and then laughed to cover it all up. 'I'm fine.'

'You're sure?'

'So sure. Come on, let's have a hot chocolate.'

Half an hour later she kissed her sister goodbye and saw her into a cab to get her back to her debating hall. She stood on the pavement and watched until the cab went round the corner, relieved that it had only been a fleeting visit. It should have been such a treat; instead it had been harder than she'd ever have imagined.

Being that uncomfortable about seeing her beloved sister shattered her. Wrong. It was just *wrong*. It should've been nothing but wonderful, but it had been a nightmare. She couldn't maintain lying to her sister—not for more than the few minutes she'd seen her for just now. She certainly couldn't lie to her sister for the rest of her life. She couldn't lie to her child. She couldn't lie to herself.

Her heart ached.

You've worked so hard for so long.

Yes, and she deserved that promotion. She'd known she did a good job.

You deserve happiness… Are you happy?

She should be happy, right? But she wasn't.

She felt trapped and increasingly afraid that her

heart was Leon's prisoner. There had to be another way. She couldn't live this lie. She couldn't lie to those she loved—to *none* of those she loved. Not even him.

'Ettie, are you okay?'

She turned to find Joel on the pavement next to her, concern on his face. 'I'm fine, thanks, Joel. I'm just going to take a walk.'

She needed time to think about how things were going to work. She didn't know what the answer was yet, but something had to change. She walked through the streets and saw the station in the distance. On automatic pilot, she caught the train, letting the familiar route soothe her. She'd not intended to go there, but when she arrived she knew it was what she needed.

Her apartment was colder than usual. Almost empty. He'd had professionals in, because all her stuff was in a few boxes. The furniture was being left for the next person who moved in. She glanced at the windowsill. Not even her herbs needed her any more. They'd already died from the few days of neglect. But it was her home. And in it she'd been honest. And happy.

She needed to be honest again and take back some control. She'd let Leon dictate everything until now. She'd been tired and overwhelmed and confused. But she wasn't now. And she knew what had to happen.

She couldn't sign that contract. She couldn't stay with him. She couldn't live that lie for the rest of her life.

It would slowly tear her apart and she couldn't do

that to herself. Because her intuitive, immediate answer to Ophelia's question had hit her hard.

Yes, she loved him.

She'd fallen in love with Leon. In love with a man who didn't love her. Again.

But this wasn't like it was with her ex. She'd never loved *him*. She'd not known what love was until Leon. Not love, nor lust, nor laughter and true companionship…for just a moment she'd had a glimpse of what might've been possible if he loved her too.

Now she looked at the emerald on her finger. It was so beautiful, but without heart. It should have heart with it—it was too stunning to be empty. She took it off and put it on the table, turning away to curl up on the old lumpy sofa. She needed to think through how she was going to be able to live with Leon in her life, but without ever having him in the way she ached for. And she was suddenly so tired, so heartsore, she just had to close her eyes and hide.

The knock on her door an hour later startled her. She checked the peephole and got even more of a shock.

'What are you doing here?' She stepped back after letting Leon in, nervously tugging her shirt when she saw his grim expression.

'Joel called. He was concerned about you.'

Why? 'How did you know where to find me?'

'Seeing as you left your phone at Cavendish, I made a lucky guess,' he said in a chilled voice. 'Joel said Ophelia visited you. Is she okay?'

'She's great. Really. So happy.'

'I'm glad.'

Ettie pressed her lips together. He didn't sound glad.

'I'm sorry if I worried you,' she said.

He didn't answer. He'd seen the ring on the table and he didn't lift his gaze from it.

'I'm not signing that contract, Leon,' she blurted, unable to hide her hurt from him any more. 'I don't expect you to pay for Ophelia's fees. I never should have accepted that offer. I can make it work some other way.'

'What are you saying, Ettie?' His expression had frozen.

She clenched her fists and tried to hold herself together. 'I allowed you to make all the decisions. It all happened so fast, I wasn't feeling well...we got carried away on a tsunami of panic and some of this wasn't necessary.'

'Wasn't necessary?' he repeated in cool disbelief, and turned to look at her hard. 'Ettie, you're pregnant.'

'Yes, and we need to make rational decisions.'

'You call walking out of work and coming back to this dump a rational decision?'

She drew in a sharp breath. He was angry with her, unused to being challenged. 'This is my home. I was happy here.'

'You're not happy at my home?'

'You swept in and took command—'

'You were *ill*,' he pointed out icily.

'You tipped my life upside down,' she shouted

back. 'It's just been so quick and I haven't had the chance to think everything through.' She needed to slow down because her alarm bells were ringing.

'What do you want?' he exploded. 'I was *trying*—'

'Yes,' she interrupted harshly. 'Trying too hard.'

He sent her a wrathful look. 'I *what*?' he muttered, outraged.

'You don't want to marry me any more than I want to marry you.'

That silenced him.

'You don't, Leon.' She rubbed her arms, suddenly cold. 'It's a calculated decision you think you have to live with. But you don't. And I can't live a lie for the rest of my life. I can't pretend to be happy when I'm not.'

'You've given us less than a week.' He was livid.

'Isn't it better to realise the mistake sooner rather than later?'

'Or maybe you should give us more time. I might be trying too hard, but you're bailing out at the first chance you've got. You've been betrayed in the past and you're letting your fears get in the way of a perfectly fine future. You think I'll walk out on you,' he added coldly. 'So you've left before I can.'

His accusation stole her breath.

'I can't do this,' she whispered. 'I can't marry you.'

She was his choice by default. They were forced together purely by the fate of a failed condom. Sure, he was offering security for her baby. Their child would want for nothing—it would have the adoration of both parents.

'You're a good guy, Leon, okay?' she said un-evenly. 'You win the honourable prize. You're a man who steps up and does the right thing. But you don't have to take it this far, okay?'

'This far?'

'I can't marry you. I can't live with you. I certainly can't sign that horrible contract and be *paid* to like you. We can just co-parent. We can make some better arrangement.'

He glared at her. 'You're saying you don't want to sleep with me any more?'

'We're only back together because of the baby. You don't really want me.'

'How can you say I don't want you when I can't keep my hands off you?' he roared and shoved those hands into his trouser pockets.

She gritted her teeth. 'That's just sex. And frankly, we're using it to paper over the cracks in this ar-rangement.'

'We what?' He dragged in a sharp breath. Then another. 'You're complaining about our sex life?'

'You use it to avoid emotional intimacy.'

He froze. 'And what do you use it for?'

She couldn't answer that. She just couldn't.

He stared at her. 'You read too much into every-thing. You attach meaning to memories that don't actually matter.'

'Don't they matter? Don't you think they impact how we both choose to live?' She stepped closer, sud-denly shaking with emotion, with how important it was to cut through to what was vitally important. And honest.

'Yes, I've been hurt before and I don't want to be hurt again,' she admitted. 'And if I stay with you, I will be. I've tried to treat this like an arrangement, but I can't. I'm not like you, I can't keep my emotions "under control", and I don't want to.' She inhaled a deep breath and forced herself to finish. 'We'll work together to take care of the baby, but being together in an empty relationship isn't right. I can't keep sleeping with you, Leon. It's destroying me.' It hurt her so much to say it, but it had to be done. 'You deserve more than this…facade. You deserve love. And so do I.'

She wanted him to find love. He deserved it after everything he'd missed out on. And she wanted to find real love for herself too. To *be* loved. While she could be everything *but* the one he truly wanted, that wasn't enough for her. She wasn't going to put herself through the heartache of being with a man who didn't really want her. Her child needed to see both its mother and its father, loved and loving. If not to each other, then to significant others when and if they appeared.

She'd tried, but she couldn't be like him. Nor was she the one for him. Because if she was he'd have recognised it already—he would have *felt* it. He would have known he didn't need that contract to bind her to him. He was a smart guy, not slow.

'Love?' he scoffed. 'There's no such thing as love. That's the rubbish of fairy tales and films. There's just reality and practicality. There's lust and there are contracts.'

And that just proved her point completely. Because

for her there *was* love. She felt it for *him*. She ached to give him everything she possibly could, but he didn't feel that way for her. She braced tightly against the painful intensity of rejection.

This is the right decision, Ettie. Right, right, right.

Leon stared at Ettie's expression in the silence that followed his outburst. Dread surged in his belly, a hideous whirlpool of horror and regret. He shouldn't have said that. He shouldn't have crushed her dreams with his icy reality. She hadn't deserved that. Yet he'd had to be honest with her.

He cleared his throat. 'We can make this work, Ettie. We *will* make it work.'

'Yes,' she nodded curtly, 'but not the way you want it to.'

He glared, waiting for her to explain.

'You might be prepared to settle, but I'm not.' She straightened. In a blink the distress was gone from her eyes. There was only determination there now.

'Settle?' The chill spread from his gut to his limbs and then—blessedly—up to his brain. Finally he could think clearly.

'I do believe in that kind of love, Leon.' She looked up at him. Emotion shadowed her eyes, but dignity shone clearly from within them. There were no tears, only resolution. 'I've fallen in love with you,' she said. 'That's why I can't stay and why I won't marry you.'

He stared, dumbstruck, as his brain short-circuited. She *what*?

'How can that possibly surprise you?' she asked

with a shake of her head. 'How could I not…? But you don't love me and that's okay.'

'You're not in love with me,' he blurted mechanically.

She was confusing it with gratitude. He was the first person to do things for her. Not betray her. Not abandon her. Not take and take and take. And she had such little experience with sex, she didn't realise it was just physical pleasure. He'd rubbed her up the right way, that was all.

'It's the lifestyle,' he said roughly.

Now her expressive eyes flashed—all anger. 'I don't fall in love with *things*, Leon. You insult me. Your contract insulted me. I'd still love you even if you were poor and lived in a cardboard box. That you felt I needed some reward for staying with you…' She shook her head.

That feeling inside roiled and burned but still he rejected what she was saying.

Her expression hardened in the face of his silence. 'You don't get to deny my feelings or my wishes. You don't get to make all the decisions.' She drew in a deep breath. 'You've found out all my other secrets—you might as well know everything. I fell in love with you probably that very first night. But you don't feel the same. You're trying to do the right thing, but it's too much to ask of you—it's obvious you don't really want to when you can't bear to reveal anything of yourself and you can't trust me for more than five minutes. And I get why, I do. You shouldn't have to open up to someone you don't care about. But don't deny what's true for me. It's painful enough. You don't want emotional intimacy with me. Fine, don't have it. But you don't get physical either. You don't get to have the cake and eat it too. You want too much from me. I can't separate it the way you do.'

She did *not* love him. He could deny that and he would. 'You barely know me.'

'I know all I need to know. Who you are is what you do. And you do loyal. Kind. Funny. Determined. Stubborn to the point of—' She broke off as her breathing hitched.

Yet it wasn't enough, was it? He'd given her everything he could and it still wasn't enough.

'You don't have to feel bad,' she added, her clear-eyed gaze narrowing on him. 'You don't have to pretend any more. You can find someone else.'

Is that what *she* wanted?

'How bloody generous of you, Ettie,' he said scathingly. 'You haven't even given this a chance. You say you love me but you can walk out just like that?' He snapped his fingers as his anger flared. 'Not much of a love really.'

Her face whitened. 'I also love *myself*. I am worthy of that job promotion. I deserve the great sex life you've shown me is possible. *You're* the one who's taught me I deserve more. Not to expect less or settle for worse. And thank you for that. But now I have to protect myself.' She lifted her chin. 'You don't love me.'

'That's not the point.' He dismissed the statement. 'It is.'

He was so furious he couldn't look at her any more. Wildly he glanced around and saw the herbs on the windowsill had become little more than a collection of musty leaves in the pots. Without her presence and care they hadn't taken long to wither and die. So typical. He felt his grip on himself slip as that monstrous crushing inside threatened to kill every last brain cell he had and render him only capable of...*what*?

Oh, his body knew what it wanted—to prove to her that she couldn't resist him again. Hell, he needed to get away before he totally lost it.

She'd completely rejected everything he'd offered. She'd rejected him.

'At the very least I can house you,' he said icily. 'Not here.' He retrieved the ring from the table. It burned his palm and he shoved it into his pocket. He stalked to the door, needing to leave before he said or did something he'd regret. 'I'll be in touch to make new arrangements.'

CHAPTER ELEVEN

Love? She wanted *love*?

Leon was living in a perpetual state of frustration. With every breath he whipped from fury to wrath and back again.

Let her go. Let her stay in her horrible, small apartment. Let her be alone and miserable if that was what she was determined to do. He was happy to have his house back to himself, right? He'd found it hard sharing with someone for the first time in his life. He'd go back to how it had been—how he liked it. Alone, independent, strong, easy.

But he paced the vast, empty space until the puppy got too tired to follow his every step. He sank onto the sofa and scooped the little guy up. The pup immediately curled into a ball on his stomach and began to snooze.

Leon had no such respite. He'd done everything he could for Ettie. He'd given her a far better home. He'd looked after her health and freed her from that financial burden, he'd recognised her worth at work. He'd had her well-being foremost in his mind. What more did she want?

But he hadn't done everything.

The inner voice repeated it—over and over. From a whisper it strengthened in volume and insistence until it was ringing incessantly in his head.

The void she'd left was huge. She'd taken more than he'd realised.

The baby. Right? It was just the baby. He reasoned his way through the bereft sensation. She was taking away his *child*. And with that recognition his anger returned in full force. He railed inwardly at her stubborn selfishness.

He'd been told so often that people would only want *things* from him. Money, mostly. Money and the kind of "doors open" access his privilege engendered. And that wisdom had proven true often enough in the past. But not this time.

He'd given everything to *her*. At least everything that was easy to give—his money, his success, his home. What was harder was what was hidden. What he didn't even want to face himself. The security she craved wasn't financial. What she'd said she wanted—needed—was emotional. And that was impossible. He didn't believe in love. He didn't even know what it was. Yet with every day that dragged, that bereft feeling only built a bigger and bigger hole inside. It wasn't the thought of the baby at all.

He put a security team back on her. He initiated all the paperwork he could think of to secure both her rights and his, ditching that damned contract he'd drawn up over that weekend to try to hold the complications at bay. But three interminable days later, he still couldn't sleep at night. Worry nagged.

He hated thinking of her being alone. He hated re-membering her words. But they echoed relentlessly—a melody to his own berating beat—dragging in loss, lust, unbearable loneliness…and at the heart of that hideous mix grew an intolerable, impossible yearn-ing.

I love you, Leon.

It was the first time in his life someone had said that to him and actually meant it. He knew, to his bones, how much she thought she'd meant it. She barely knew him but she believed her words. He'd been unable to. And he'd been right because in the next second she'd snatched them back again by re-jecting everything he'd offered. By rejecting *him*. She didn't love him enough to stay. She didn't even want his damn money. She was so determined to be inde-pendent, all because he couldn't what—wail on about his past? Open up to her? Love her?

Didn't she understand that he couldn't? He didn't know how.

He knew she wouldn't deny him access to his child. She'd just denied him access to *her*. She'd taken her company, her attention, her presence from him. And somehow that was the worst. He couldn't stand it. Nor could he fathom *why* it was so horrendous.

So he did what he'd always done: he fought for con-trol. He isolated himself. He worked round the clock. And he avoided all contact with anyone at Cavendish House. They'd be Team Ettie all the way. He didn't blame them. He understood their loyalty.

He also knew Ettie needed to be loved. That was

why she worked for everyone—she ached for any kind of affection. She didn't realise that all those people cared about her without her having to work for it; it was because of the person she was—sunny, generous, interested, enthusiastic about everything in life...

And he'd been stupid enough to tell her he didn't believe in love.

He sat on the floor of his home and rubbed the puppy's ears and finally admitted to himself that he was a coward. More than that, he was a jerk. He'd not accepted what she'd offered. He'd not even acknowledged the truth of it.

The fourth morning it was worse. He couldn't stand it any more. The isolation and gaping hole inside widened with every angry second that ticked by and today it was an actual physical pain. And that was when it finally hit—it wasn't *rage* he felt. It was *hurt*.

Deep, incurable hurt. He was so vulnerable. She'd prised layers of protection and defence open and then she'd struck him hard.

Not even the unconditional trust of the little puppy soothed him. The dog just made it worse, because he made caring—adoration—seem easy. Not to Leon it wasn't. He closed his eyes and leaned against the cool window overlooking his immaculate garden.

Ettie had given him the smallest, tantalising glimpse of something he'd never imagined. When she'd said she was in love with him, he'd had that heart-busting vision of a small family filled with fun and laughter and passion. A family that was *together*. The kind of family he'd never had.

In his childhood family there'd been no honesty. No laughter. No love. Nothing but cold cruelty from his mother. And when he'd tried to talk to his father, the older man had shut down. Dismissed his truth. Silenced him.

But hadn't Leon just done the exact same thing to Ettie? Hadn't he shut down and closed off contact? He'd refused to even acknowledge the problem, let alone try to resolve it.

While he'd silenced her, Ettie had never silenced him. She'd let him speak. She'd wanted him to speak more. She hadn't judged him for his words, she'd just accepted him.

Bile rose in his throat. He did not want to be like his father. And he sure as hell refused to be like his mother. Why had he thought any of what that woman had wanted was okay?

Never show weakness. Not anger. Not fear. No tears. No laughter.

Even when he'd learned to bury his emotions, his mother hadn't loved him. Nothing he could've done could have changed that. She'd taught him all the wrong things. And he'd been so busy fighting for those tangible signs of success, he'd not stopped to see how much he was missing. How much his mother had actually *won*—because here he was, living a life so isolated, he might as well be back in that cupboard she'd locked him in.

Ettie was the one who was right. Expressing emotions *wasn't* the same as losing control of them. And even if he did lose control? What then? What was the worst that could happen? The worst had *already* happened.

Ettie had left him.

And now here he was in his huge house—isolated, cold and stuck in the emotional stunting of his past. He'd thought he was over it, that he was free of that pain. But he wasn't beyond it at all. His own beautiful big house offered no more comfort or companionship than that dark, hideous cupboard of his childhood torment.

That constriction inside—the tight-bound hard knot inside him—finally loosened. And it hurt like hell. But he would *not* be an absent father to this child—physically or emotionally. He had to make more of an effort because he didn't want his child turning out like him. He gazed sightlessly over the garden as he fully realised the painful, amazing truth. That knot inside—he'd hardened it, tried to cover it up, because it was more than a crusted nugget of hope. It was his heart.

Ettie had breathed life into it, blowing on old embers to bring back a flame. His inner fire was flickering now but it needed more fuel.

While he'd do anything to protect his baby, what was even more incredible—wonderful and terrifying—was that he'd fallen so completely in love with its mother. It wasn't just the physical contact, but everything she brought with her. Her smile had put sparkle into his life. He simply wanted to put his battered heart into her hands and be with her. And he wanted to care for her in *all* ways. Her words hadn't just unsettled him, they'd also left him raw. She had a power he'd never have believed it would be possible for anyone to have over him. He was still a little angry with her for that. And yet he knew he too had the power to gravely hurt her. He already had. But he'd never do that again.

He thought back to that very first night—to the way she'd run away the next morning, too scared to even look him in the eye. Braced for rejection, for betrayal, she'd been so certain she was going to be hurt. She'd run because he'd not given her what she needed.

But in order to get her back he had to open up in the way he'd told himself he never would, that he'd never thought he *could*. Heartache forced him forward. There was no alternative, no getting over this. The gap she'd left in his life was crippling.

He'd thought he had it all. He'd thought he was invincible. But he had nothing of real value. Now he'd finally realised, he knew he had to do something about it.

There was action and there was *action*.

CHAPTER TWELVE

It was moving day.

Ettie looked around her little flat. Not much had changed in the days since she'd left Leon and come back to live alone.

He'd been in touch as promised, but only via paperwork. Formal, bloodless documentation offering her an apartment in Cavendish House to make it easy for her to work and be near to his home. It didn't matter how near or far from her he was, he still killed her heart, but she couldn't be under the same roof as him, couldn't sleep with him any more, and that would happen if she stayed at his house. He didn't love her and that was fine, but to remain and give everything of herself would slowly destroy her.

At least Leon travelled for work. She'd have moments of pure respite. Those urges in the smallest hours of the morning, to run to him, to tell him again that she loved him, to try to convince him to love her...she could ignore those. If she ignored them for long enough, surely they'd disappear. Surely she'd done the right thing?

But doubts niggled. Should she have fought harder for him?

Only then she remembered her past. Hadn't she been humiliated enough? The man didn't love her. No man had ever loved her. Not her father. Not her ex. Not Leon.

Snap out of it, Ettie.

The removal van was due in five minutes. She'd had very little to do—just repacked those few belongings she'd got out.

Someone knocked on the door. She checked the peephole. The guy's cap was pulled low but had the removal logo on it. He was early. Of course, anyone hired by Leon would be efficient in the extreme.

She opened the door, knowing the security guard stationed along from her flat would have already vetted him. But it wasn't the removal man. It was Leon himself.

She stared, her tongue stuck to the roof of her mouth. She'd never seen him this casually dressed. She'd pretty much only seen him either in a suit or naked. Now he was in black jeans, black T-shirt— and both fitted him lovingly. The effect of his outfit was…*appallingly inappropriate.* She clenched her jaw and her fists, furious for her basic reaction to him. *Every time.*

He totalled her senses.

'I need to be able to help you, Ettie.' He shifted on his feet and broke the silence. 'Don't you think?'

That's all he wanted to do?

Unable to speak, she nodded and stood aside so he could enter. She had to be stronger than this.

He was holding a tray she'd not seen through the peephole. 'I brought you these.'

A trio of little plants in pretty pots. Fresh herbs to replace the ones that had died.

'Housewarming present for your new apartment,' he explained in her silence. 'I noticed your other ones hadn't survived your absence.'

Of course. He noticed everything. He'd even got the exact right herbs—thyme, chives, basil. Her battered heart burst apart that little bit more. But it was a peace offering and she could be adult enough to accept it, couldn't she?

'Thank you,' she said awkwardly as he put the plants on the old dining table.

He didn't pick up one of the stacked boxes. Instead he looked across the small space to her, his expression more serious than ever. It should have been impossible.

'I'm sorry.' His words spilled suddenly into the taut silence. Uneven and harsh, like sharp pebbles tossed with piercing aim.

Was that what he'd come to offer? An apology? Her heart cranked open again, seeping pain and pure disappointment. She should appreciate the gesture, but she found she wasn't quite ready to be *friends* with him yet. Too soon. Too sore.

She blinked rapidly, tried to pull herself together enough to offer a polite smile. Could he just shift the boxes now? But he was standing there—as still as still, his expression unreadable, his eyes as dark as his T-shirt.

'I don't know what love really is, Ettie. I only know what it isn't and I couldn't let that happen to you. It's why I thought I should—could—let you go. I never wanted you to be unhappy.'

Yes, she knew he hadn't meant to hurt her. He'd only tried to do the right thing. Now, could he *please* pick up a box?

'Ettie?' He paused. 'Please look at me.'

He asked so softly and she couldn't resist. This was the problem; she didn't think she could *ever* resist. Not for long. She wasn't ready for this yet.

He was paler than usual. Intense. Rigid. Her eyes filled because he was trying to open up and be honest and she could see the cost of that effort. She could see the desperation in him. Because he knew he'd hurt her and he didn't like that. He might be bossy, but he was kind, and that broke her heart all over again. 'Leon—'

'No. Let me finish. Hell, start. I'm making a mess of it.' He rubbed his hand through his hair, frustration leaping from him. 'It's taken me a bit to realise you weren't rejecting *me*. You thought you were doing the right thing for me. For the baby. And for you. Because you wanted more than what I was offering. You were right to want that.'

Not the money, the lifestyle, the security. No, she'd wanted something far more precious from him.

'I've always been unwilling to share space with anyone, share anything much. I didn't know how.'

He stood still but Ettie could see the faint trembling of his fingers and she waited. She couldn't have spoken if she'd tried.

'I have that massive house because it made me feel free. I thought we'd hardly be aware of each other in there, but somehow you filled it,' he said. 'I didn't know it at the time, but I've never been as scared in all my life as those few days when you were living with me. And then you left.' He puffed out a long, pained breath. 'And now I've finally worked out what it was I'd been so afraid of. It was that. You *leaving.*' He paused. 'Having you with me was like a dream, and I didn't want to wake up and find you gone. Not again.'

Ettie couldn't move, couldn't open her mouth, not even to release the moan building in her chest. She hurt so much—for him, for her. And the fragile hope that was mounting within was too much to bear.

'I didn't recognise what I was feeling,' he said. 'I just didn't know, Ettie. I've never had it before. Never felt it.' He stepped nearer to her, his eyes blazing almost black with intensity. 'You were right. I buried myself—us—in sex. I had this driving need to get closer to you. It's so good, but that's because it's *not* just physical, Ettie.' His voice lifted. 'It never was. I think back to that first day. I've never been as intrigued by anyone. You were passionate and fiery and sweet and kind. But the thing is, you do lovely things for everyone and I doubted that I was all that special—'

'I don't sleep with just anyone,' she interrupted harshly.

'I know.' He lifted his shoulders and then let them

fall in a slight, helpless movement of concession. 'You slipped under my armour without my even realising I had armour on. And then I was vulnerable. I didn't like that, Ettie. Uncertainty is hideous.' He dragged in another breath. 'The trouble is, I don't know *how* to give you what's in here.' He pressed his fist to his chest. 'All I knew was that I wanted you to be free and happy, to fly and have all the things I thought you hadn't had… Before these last few days, I never stopped to wonder *why* I wanted that for you but it's since become obvious. I wanted what's best for you, because I've fallen in love with you. I wanted you to have everything…' His voice petered out and he stood there, alone and exposed.

'I just wanted *you*.' Ettie's throat was so tight she could only whisper as her hope overflowed her wounded heart. '*You* were my pick, my special thing just for me. That first night and ever since, all I've ever wanted was *you*.'

The expression on his face crumbled her defences. He looked torn—somewhere between touched and hopeful and terrified.

'I love you and I'm not going to stop loving you.' Her voice shook. 'But—'

'You think I'm only here because of the baby.' He gazed at her, reading her own vulnerability, her own limiting fears. 'No. Our future was set the second I clapped eyes on you. One night was never going to be enough. But you worked for me and you were shy and I was processing how to get around that when we found out…you were pregnant. That changed everything and I think I just went on auto—instinct telling me what needed to happen and what I really wanted… And that's you—*all* of you and *all* the love you have to give.' He paused. His voice was strained. 'I'm so greedy, Ettie. I want you in my life. I don't want to let you go. I'm *not* going to let you go. And I refuse to regret the circumstances that brought us back together. I can't wait until we meet our baby. I love you.' He shook his head as he repeated it beneath his breath.

She put her hand on his lips and stopped him. 'You deserve to have all the love.' Her eyes watered.

'But how do I show you? How do I make you happy?'

His admission—letting her see his vulnerability—touched her more than anything.

She shook her head. 'You just do—just *you*. Listening to me, laughing with me, loving me. It's not pity. It's compassion. It's understanding.'

He gazed so hard into her eyes it was as though he was drinking her words in and was desperately trying to understand, to believe…

'You don't even realise you're doing it,' she muttered, half marvelling. 'Why do you think I fell in love with you? I took one look and wanted you. Even when I thought you were a heartless brute about to condemn Toby, I still felt that physical pull. But I fell in love with you that night—you let me see your smile, you let me in enough to laugh with me, and it was just magic. You were funny and smart and you noticed what I needed before I realised it myself. You *see* me. You know how to care, Leon. It's innate in you.'

The stark emotion in his eyes melted her.

'You're also completely bossy,' she couldn't help teasing.

He didn't hide his smile then. 'What, you mean I'm not perfect?'

'How boring would that be?' She cupped his jaw, reading the tension lingering in his eyes. 'Just talk to me—about anything. Nothing. Everything. I don't need grand gestures, Leon, or fancy dates. It's the everyday things you already do so well.' She pointed at the herbs. 'See? You notice. You care.'

He frowned and put out a dismissive hand. 'That was just—'

'Thoughtful,' she interrupted. 'You did it because you were thinking of me.'

'I think of you all the time,' he muttered huskily.

She stilled because in that moment she truly, finally, completely believed him. It had been the simplest, most heartfelt declaration she'd ever heard.

'Why are you crying?' He pulled her against his chest as her face crumpled and she sobbed.

'Because I'm happy.' She clung to him, needing to feel his heat and strength. 'I love you, Leon.'

He was here. And he was hers.

'I love you too.' He cradled her gently, stroking his hand down her back as she cried out the days of loneliness and heartache. 'I want everything with you— laughter, love, babies, puppies.'

She gurgled with watery laughter but hugged him

hard. 'You were right too,' she said softly. 'I was afraid of going for what I wanted—of making a mistake again—so I ran. It's been so awful. All I wanted was you. And I was terrified that you didn't want me.'

Despite all the kisses that had gone before, this felt like their first. In that magical moment just before contact, when breath mingled and eyes locked, that was nerves and excitement, happiness and wonder. Ettie understood his stillness for what it was—the remnants of fear, anxiety and loss leaving them both. This time their sensuality wasn't to avoid emotional intimacy, but to enhance it. And so swiftly, it flared. Incandescently.

'*Glykia mou.*'

He pushed her clothes aside. Kisses touched skin the second it was bared. When she couldn't stand any more he took her down to the floor, into his embrace. He lifted her onto his lap so she straddled him. Face to face, eye to eye. Back in the light where there was no hiding anything. He held her, helped her slide on him until he was buried as deep as possible. More tears trickled at the sudden, exquisite fulfilment. Sealed tightly to him, staring deep into his eyes, she'd never felt this close to anyone. Never as secure…

And never as *hot*.

A glint of amusement sparked in his eye as he slid his hand down to lightly stroke right where she was most sensitive.

'I'm trying to slow down,' she complained with a moan of delight, and leaned closer to kiss his gorgeous mouth.

'Why?' he muttered against her with pure temptation. 'We can always do it again. We can love each other like this every day for the rest of our lives.'

Every nerve curled in unendurable elation. She trembled in his arms as her physical and emotional reaction to his promise consumed her. He loved her so hard and she loved him right back.

For a long time, they remained breathless in the blissful safety of that loving embrace.

He reached out a long arm and grabbed his jeans from the heap of clothes on the floor and pulled something sparkly out of his pocket. 'Is it too soon to put this back where it belongs?'

She stared at the ring and then back up at him. Her heart galloped faster than it had only moments ago when she'd been recovering from the most intense orgasm of her life.

'We can always get another if you don't like it, but I thought the emerald matched your eyes...you probably didn't notice.' His voice trailed off and he fell silent.

She felt the acceleration of his heart beneath her hand. 'I noticed,' she breathed.

'You did?' His face lit up.

Heart overflowing, she lifted her hand so he could slide the ring back on her finger.

'Will you marry me, Ettie Roberts?' he asked unevenly.

'Yes,' she whispered as she stared into his eyes. 'It's beautiful.' And now it had heart; now it glittered even more brilliantly than before.

'It's for real, Ettie,' he promised, husky and true. 'It's for always.'

Bathed in love, she laced her fingers through his.

'Let's go home,' he said. 'Basil will be wondering where we are.'

'You named the puppy Basil?' She leaned against him and laughed with pure, infectious joy. 'Yes. Let's go home to him.'

Together.

* * * * *

If you enjoyed
Pregnant by the Commanding Greek,
you're sure to enjoy these other stories
by Natalie Anderson!

Claiming His Convenient Fiancée
Princess's Pregnancy Secret
The King's Captive Virgin
Awakening His Innocent Cinderella

Available now!

COMING NEXT MONTH FROM

HARLEQUIN Presents®

Available May 21, 2019

#3721 THE SHEIKH CROWNS HIS VIRGIN
Billionaires at the Altar
by Lynne Graham

When Zoe is kidnapped, she's saved by Raj—an exiled desert prince. The attraction between them is instant! Yet her rescue comes with a price: to avoid a scandal, Zoe *must* become Raj's virgin bride...

#3722 SHOCK HEIR FOR THE KING
Secret Heirs of Billionaires
by Clare Connelly

Frankie is shocked when Matt, the stranger she gave her innocence to, reappears. Now she's in for the biggest shock of all—he's actually *King* Matthias! And to claim his heir, he demands Frankie become his queen!

#3723 GREEK'S BABY OF REDEMPTION
One Night With Consequences
by Kate Hewitt

When brooding billionaire Alex needs a wife to secure his business, his housekeeper, Milly, agrees. But their wedding night sparks an unexpected fire... Could Milly—and his unborn child—be the key to Alex's redemption?

#3724 UNTOUCHED UNTIL HER ULTRA-RICH HUSBAND
by Dani Collins

To avoid destitution, Luli needs outrageously wealthy Gabriel's help. The multi-billionaire's solution? He'll secure both their futures by marrying her! But after sweeping Luli into his luxurious world, Gabriel discovers the chemistry with his untouched wife is *priceless*...

HPCNM0519RA

#3725 A SCANDALOUS MIDNIGHT IN MADRID
Passion in Paradise
by Susan Stephens

A moonlit encounter tempts Sadie all the way to Alejandro's castle...and into his bed! But their night of illicit pleasure soon turns Sadie into Spain's most scandalous headline: *Pregnant with Alejandro's baby!*

#3726 UNTAMED BILLIONAIRE'S INNOCENT BRIDE
Conveniently Wed!
by Caitlin Crews

To prevent a scandal, Lauren needs to find reclusive Dominik—her boss's estranged brother—and convince him to marry her! As Dominik awakens her long-dormant desire, will Lauren accept that their hunger can't be denied?

#3727 CLAIMING HIS REPLACEMENT QUEEN
Monteverre Marriages
by Amanda Cinelli

Khalil's motivation for marriage is politics, not passion. Yet a sizzling encounter with his soon-to-be queen, Cressida, changes everything. And the desire innocent Cressida ignites is too hot to resist...

#3728 REUNITED BY THE GREEK'S VOWS
by Andie Brock

Kate is stunned when ex-fiancé, Nikos, storms back into her life—and demands they marry! Desperate to save her company, she agrees. But what these heated adversaries don't anticipate is that their still-smoldering flame will explode into irresistible passion...

YOU CAN FIND MORE INFORMATION ON UPCOMING HARLEQUIN® TITLES, FREE EXCERPTS AND MORE AT WWW.HARLEQUIN.COM.

HPCNM0519RB

You told me what you were worth, Luli. Act like you believe it.

She had been acting. The whole time. Still was, especially as a handful of designers whose names she knew from Mae's glossy magazines behaved with deference as they welcomed her to a private showroom complete with catwalk.

She had to fight back laughing with incredulity as they offered her champagne, caviar, even a pedicure.

"I—" She glanced at Gabriel, expecting him to tell them she aspired to model and should be treated like a clotheshorse, not royalty.

"A full wardrobe," he said. "Top to bottom, morning to night, office to evening. Do what you can overnight, then send the rest to my address in New York."

"Mais bien sûr, monsieur," the couturier said without a hint of falter in her smile. "Our pleasure."

"Gabriel—" Luli started to protest as the women scattered.

"You remember what I said about this?" He tapped the wallet that held her phone. "I need you to stay on brand."

"Reflect who you are?"

"Yes."

"Who are you?" she asked ruefully. "I only met you ten minutes ago."

"I'm a man who doesn't settle for anything less than the best." He touched her chin. "The world is going to have a lot of questions about why we married. Give them an answer."

His words roused the competitor who still lurked inside her. She wanted to prove to the world she was worthy to be his wife. Maybe she wanted to prove her worth to him, too. Definitely she longed to prove something to herself.

Either way, she made sure those long-ago years of preparation paid off. She had always been ruthless in evaluating her own shortcomings and knew how to play to her strengths. She might not be trying to win a crown today, but she hadn't been then, either. She'd been trying to win the approval of a woman who hadn't deserved her idolatry.

She pushed aside those dark memories and clung instead to the education she had gained in those difficult years.

"That neckline will make my shoulders look narrow," she said, making quick up-and-down choices. "The sweetheart style is better, but no ruffles at my hips. Don't show me yellow. Tangerine is better. A more verdant green. That one is too pale." In her head, she was sectioning out the building blocks of a cohesive stage presence. Youthful, but not too trendy. Sensual, but not overtly sexual. Charismatic without being showy.

"Something tells me I'm not needed," Gabriel said twenty minutes in and rose to leave. "We'll go for dinner in three hours." He glanced to the couturier. "And return in the morning for another fitting."

"Parfait. Merci, monsieur." Her smile was calm, but the way people were bustling told Luli how big a deal this was. How big a deal Gabriel was.

The women took her measurements while showing her unfinished pieces that only needed hemming or minimal tailoring so she could take them immediately.

"You'll be up all night," Luli murmured to one of the seamstresses.

The young woman moved quickly, but not fast enough for her boss, who kept crying, *"Vite! Vite!"*

"I'm sorry to put you through this," Luli added.

"Pas de problème. Monsieur Dean is a treasured client. It's our honor to provide your trousseau." She clamped her teeth on a pin between words. "Do you know where he's taking you for dinner? We should choose that dress next, so I can work on the alterations while you have your hair and makeup done. It must be fabulous. The world will be watching."

She would be presented publicly as his wife, Luli realized with a hard thump in her heart.

Don't miss
Untouched Until Her Ultra-Rich Husband.
Available June 2019 wherever
Harlequin® Presents books and ebooks are sold.

www.Harlequin.com

HPEXP0519

HARLEQUIN *Presents*®

**Coming next month—
a seductive Spanish romance!**

**In *A Scandalous Midnight in Madrid* by Susan Stephens,
Sadie is shocked by the red-hot connection she feels when
she encounters the aristocratic Spanish billionaire.
But what's even more shocking, is when she discovers
that she's pregnant with his baby...**

Dedicated chef Sadie's life is changed forever by an
intense moonlit encounter in Madrid with infamous
Alejandro de Alegon. The sizzling anticipation he sparks
tempts virgin Sadie all the way to his Spanish castle...and
into his bed! She's never known anything like the wild passion
Alejandro unleashes. But when Sadie discovers their night of
illicit pleasure had consequences, she becomes Spain's biggest
headline: scandalously pregnant with Alejandro's baby!

A Scandalous Midnight in Madrid

Passion in Paradise

Available June 2019

HPBPA0519